ENCORE

ENCORE

ALEXIS KOETTING

FIVE STAR
A part of Gale, Cengage Learning

GALE
CENGAGE Learning®

Farmington Hills, Mich • San Francisco • New York • Waterville, Maine
Meriden, Conn • Mason, Ohio • Chicago

GALE
CENGAGE Learning®

LIBRARY OF CONGRESS CATALOGING-IN-PUBLICATION DATA

Koetting, Alexis.
    Encore / Alexis Koetting. — First edition.
        pages cm
    ISBN 978-1-4328-3123-3 (hardcover) — ISBN 1-4328-3123-2 (hardcover) — ISBN 978-1-4328-3124-0 (ebook) — ISBN 1-4328-3124-0 (ebook)
        1. Actresses—Fiction. 2. Murder—Investigation—Fiction. I. Title.
    PR9199.4.K595E63 2015
    813'.6—dc23   2015008343

First Edition. First Printing: August 2015
Find us on Facebook– https://www.facebook.com/FiveStarCengage
Visit our website– http://www.gale.cengage.com/fivestar/
Contact Five Star™ Publishing at FiveStar@cengage.com

Printed in the United States of America
1 2 3 4 5 6 7 19 18 17 16 15

For Lou, who loved a good book and whom I loved
very much.

ACKNOWLEDGMENTS

Oh, my goodness, this has been a long road from the writing of the first sentence to getting it to you, the reader. Along the way, I have been blessed by so many who have shared their expertise, provided information, and offered encouragement and inspiration.

At the forefront of these amazing people is my champion extraordinaire, Jo Grossman, for whom there are simply not enough pages or words to express my gratitude.

I would like to extend a special thank-you to Detective Sergeant Brett Flynn at the Major Crime Unit of the Niagara Regional Police Service and Acting Sergeant Steve Petersen of the Hamilton Regional Police for providing a sneak peek into police life and policy.

In addition to being wonderful friends, Micheal Querin, Gabrielle Jones, and Peter Millard helped to bring the Shaw Festival to life on these pages.

Thanks to Gary Earl Ross for sharing resources and advice about mystery writing and to Uncle Ken for demystifying the legalese.

Thanks to my reading team: Steve and Colleen Allen, Ron Barry, Deborah Drakeford, Angie Gei, Mary Koetting, Barbara O'Keefe, Anne Putnam, and Jamie Williams, for trucking through the first draft, and for offering wonderfully thoughtful criticism and feedback.

Acknowledgments

I am ever so grateful for my editor, Deni Dietz, and everyone at Five Star for helping to make *Encore* the best it could be.

Thanks to my parents for cheering louder than anyone when I told them the book was being published and for their constant belief in me and enthusiasm for everything I do—well, most things ☺.

Special nuzzles and snuggles go to Grady-the-Great, who, in an attempt to make the book entirely about Moustache, provided endless inspiration.

And, finally, to my love, for talking through my moments of writer's block, for laughing and crying in all the right places, and for making sure the time that was supposed to be spent writing was spent writing rather than playing solitaire. This could never have happened without him.

The word *encore* means again; once more. It refers to a second achievement that surpasses the first.
In the theatre, it is used as a call for a repeat performance.

CHAPTER 1

He sat on my stomach, trembling and breathing heavily through his open mouth. My eyes fought against the weight of sleep, straining to see in the darkness. A flash of lightning illuminated the room and gave my still-sleeping brain a clue as to my whereabouts, while the roar of thunder that followed jolted my other senses to immediate attention. A storm raged with such ferocity that even my little cottage was quaking in fear. No wonder I'd been sleeping so soundly.

Unfortunately, thunderstorms were not a comfort to everyone and, as if hoisting his thirty-plus-pound self onto my stomach was not enough, the canine love of my life, a cross between Benji and the Shaggy D.A, swatted my face with a furry beige paw.

"Come here, Moustache," I said through a yawn, reaching out my arms and drawing him close to me.

I felt his body relax and heard his breathing slow. Wrapping myself around the dog, I nuzzled my face into the back of his neck. Moustache gave a little groan, a warning that he was there under special circumstances and I'd better not push my luck. However, another clap of thunder sent him wiggling closer to me and, within moments, he was snoring gently.

I woke to the sound of a distant siren. My clock was flashing. Moustache was on his bed on the floor. I leaned over the side of the bed and ruffled his ear. Moustache looked up at me with

11

sleepy eyes and leapt onto the bed and rolled onto his back for the belly rub he had long since manipulated into our morning routine. When he'd had enough, he jumped off the bed and trotted out of the room, anxious to explore his new surroundings and stake his claim. I heard him jump onto the chair in the living room that gave him the best view of the street and bark a bark I was sure could be heard several houses down. I knew this particular yowl to mean either the presence of a squirrel or a Golden Retriever.

I had my own battle to wage today against the unpacked boxes that filled the cottage that only a day and a half ago had become my "home." As far as furnished rentals went, it was better than fine. The furniture was in good condition, albeit a little dated. The place had been cared for and outfitted with everything one might need to live comfortably for nine months. The exterior of the cottage had character but the interior was pretty neutral—waiting for some of my own belongings to gussy it up and give it that lived in, loved look. However, unlike the dog, I was nowhere near as anxious to get started and, instead, threw the covers over my head and slept for another ten minutes.

The storm had certainly been busy while the town slept. Looking out the kitchen window, I could see the backyard was littered with branches and one of the trees had been uprooted. Moustache was happily picking up from where the storm had left off, digging feverishly, kicking up bits of mud and bark, which ended up on his back rather than the ground behind him. Rolling my eyes, I turned my attention away from Moustache, determined to enjoy a bit more of the morning before bathing the dog, a task that would no doubt be inevitable given his abundance of fur.

I took a deep swallow of green tea—I had given up coffee only recently after buying into some hype about green tea helping one to lose weight. I knew I was a perfectly healthy weight, but in show business an actress can never be too thin, and the insecurity about my curves was always rearing its ugly head. The tea was growing on me. And whether or not the weight loss thing was working, I was able to convince myself I could see enough of a difference to keep up with the trend.

I took another sip and surveyed the cardboard that contained my life. It amazed me that thirty-some years could be packed away into a dozen or so boxes. Of course, this said nothing of the scores of emotional baggage that were, just as neatly, packed away. Knowing the baggage of the cardboard variety would be much easier to deal with I tore the tape off a box labeled BOOKS and began sorting the cookbooks. In the backyard, Moustache barked.

His barking became more and more incessant. I hurried to the back door. Moustache was staring into the hole he and the storm had helped to create, intent on something out of my line of vision.

"Moustache?"

He looked at me, then back to the hole. Slipping on my Crocs, I walked out into the crisp March morning.

"Moo! Come here!"

More barking, no coming. Upon reaching the dog, I leaned over to grab his collar and caught a glimpse of Moustache's buried treasure.

CHAPTER 2

Moments after the first police car arrived on the scene, windows up and down the street filled with watchful eyes, peeking around drapes, drawing more attention to themselves in their efforts to be inconspicuous. By the time the yellow police tape had gone up around my property, my neighbors were standing on their front lawns, mugs of coffee in hand, trading chatter and speculation.

While the crowd outside grew, so did the crowd inside my little cottage. Every room was occupied by someone in one official capacity or another, traipsing their muddy selves through rooms that, in my mind, had no bearing on the investigation. I was relieved most of my things were still packed away and in no danger of falling victim to the muck and dust that began to settle as police officers, forensic examiners, detectives, and the like tracked more and more of the outside in.

Moustache was sitting on the kitchen table, surveying the goings-on with such intent focus that even if I had dangled a squirrel in front of him, I don't think he would have paid it much mind.

"So this is the great hero?" said a young detective, entering the kitchen.

I smiled in spite of my irritation at yet another pair of filthy shoes adding to the mosaic of footprints that already covered my floor.

"This is Moo-STASH," I said, emphasizing the French

pronunciation of the dog's name.

We had adopted each other in Montreal and I felt the dog should hold on to some of his French-Canadian heritage. He'd been one of several dogs from a local shelter brought to a film set I was working on to provide background activity at a would-be dog park. He quickly became a favorite of the cast and crew with his lush tail wagging eagerly in the air and his mouth in a constant smile. He was a puppy then, a ball of beige fluff, and the moment he laid his head against my leg, I knew there was no way the dog would be returning to the shelter. The handler told me Moustache had been left one night and that nothing was known of his breeding or history. Not even his name. To me, his name was obvious.

The detective held out his hand for Moustache to sniff before scratching the dog's ears. I instinctively checked out his left hand. No ring. This was a nasty habit I'd assumed in recent years whenever I met a man. One I blamed entirely on my biological clock.

He was not attractive in the Hollywood sense of the word, but was certainly pleasant to look at. His fair hair was only just beginning to thin and was speckled with grey, although he couldn't have been much older than me. It appeared he had spent a great deal of time and product giving his hair that tousled look, popular among the David Beckhams of the world. A little insecure about the grey, perhaps. Or the thinning.

"Detective Sergeant Andre Jeffers," said the man, removing his hand from the dog and holding it out to me.

Moustache gave a huff and a snort, jumped off the table and trotted out of the room.

"Bella James."

"Ah, Detective Samuel," he said, "we meet at last."

The laugh that escaped me came right from my gut. I'd played Detective Emma Samuel in the Montreal crime series

Port Authority for seven seasons before it went off the air. After the series ended, I moved to Toronto, and spent over a year trying to get out of Emma's shadow. Directors and casting agents seemed to forget I was an actress able to play something other than an Emma Samuel type. Finally, on the advice of my agent, I decided to take a break from the world of film and TV and focus on theatre, where I was sure to find more of a challenge. A few phone calls and a few meetings later, I found myself packing up, yet again, and moving to Niagara-on-the-Lake to perform for the Shaw Festival.

"You watched the show," I said and laughed again.

"Oh yeah! We'd have it on at the station and make fun of all the things you guys do wrong."

"Nice."

"So, what? You missed the show so you started digging around for some real drama?" Jeffers teased.

"Jeffers!" a voice yelled from the yard. "If you don't have the balls to look at a dead body, put on your stilettos and get your sorry ass over to traffic services with the other humps and let us real cops do our jobs!"

Jeffers' face reddened. "Staff Sergeant Skip Raines. My boss."

"He seems nice," I said.

Jeffers laughed. "I'm sorry about him. That was really . . ." A disbelieving shake of the head expressed what words could not.

"It's fine," I said, smiling reassuringly. "I've got a thick skin. You should read some of my reviews."

"I don't even know what he's doing here. He retires the end of the year. Everyone's counting down the minutes. It's just that . . ."

"Just what?"

"Let's just say if I'm going to have any kind of future in Major Crimes, I need to impress the hell out of him."

"Jeffers!"

"Starting now. It was nice to meet you, Ms. James."

"You, too," I said to his back as he slipped out the sliding door into the yard and became one of the crowd.

CHAPTER 3

After being questioned by Jeffers and Prince Charming about what I knew—how the remains were discovered; did I have any idea who the victim was; how long have I been at this residence; did I know the previous owners?—I was finally free to go. With my cottage completely taken over by what looked like the entire Niagara police force and Moustache fast asleep on the bed, I decided a little fresh air might offer a welcome respite from what had become of my morning.

While I had managed to get myself dressed and my mousy brown hair into a ponytail, I had done little more than splash water on my face and brush my teeth. I considered myself to be somewhat attractive but not one of those naturally beautiful women all other women hate, so I always tried to give my appearance a bit of effort if I was going to be seen in public. Although already mortified that Niagara's finest had caught me with my home face on, I swallowed my pride, pulled a fleece poncho over my head and stepped out into what was shaping up to be a beautiful March day.

It had been several hours since the police had arrived and I was surprised to see that the crowd of curious onlookers had stuck with it. Someone had even gone so far as to make sandwiches. Since age eighteen, I had lived in neighborhoods where people minded their own business and respected one another's anonymity. I could see from the gathering outside that Niagara-on-the-Lake was no such community. I began to question what moment of insanity had led me to accept the contract that had plopped me into the middle of all this familiarity.

"You poor dear!" a voice said and all neighborly conversation stopped.

I turned to see a diminutive woman shuffling toward me. I placed her in her mid- to late seventies. She moved quickly, albeit shakily, and unlike the rest of the neighbors on the street who had simply put boots and coats on over their loungewear, she was fully dressed underneath her winter layers, and had even taken the time to rouge her cheeks and add a pale shade of blue to her eyelids.

As soon as she spoke, all eyes turned to me and a barrage of questions, sympathetic murmurs, and detective-wannabe-theories were hurled in my direction. A sandwich and a cup of hot chocolate were thrust into my hands. I knew I was being buttered up for information and, as my stomach rumbled, I didn't care.

"Now let's not terrify the poor girl. She's already been through quite an ordeal, no doubt," the old woman said. "My dear, I'm Erna Weins. I live in the blue cottage there." She indicated the bungalow directly across the road from my own small house.

It was not only blue, it was robin's egg blue with shutters the color of butter cream. A cat of the same color—the cream not the blue—lounged on the ledge of the larger of the two front windows.

I introduced myself. Some recognized my name; others did not.

"So, what is it? A body?" asked a balding, middle-aged man puffing out his chest like a peacock and surveying the group with an air of superiority.

"Yeah," I offered, through a bite of ham and Swiss.

"Really?" asked Erna Weins with wide eyes.

"At least part of one."

"Oh, my God." Erna swallowed and reached for the hand of the woman next to her.

"Well, who is it?" asked the peacock.

"Oh, for crying out loud, Ralph, the girl just moved in. She doesn't know anybody around here." Turning to me with a smile, a woman said, "Hi, I'm Linda Yellman, Ralph's wife. We're in the green house at the end of the street." She offered her hand but settled for a nod and a smile as mine were otherwise occupied. "I loved you in that show," she added in a quick whisper, starstruck.

"You could at least tell us if it was male or female," Ralph said, continuing his interrogation. I shook my head. "Any discernible markings? The state of decomp?"

"Ralph thinks he knows everything because he watches CSI. Don't mind him," Linda said.

"I'm no expert, and quite frankly, I don't even know what I'm allowed to tell you," I said, "but the bones looked like they'd been there for quite a while."

"Ah, it's probably just some bones from the war," Ralph said dismissively. "This area was once a battleground, you know." I didn't. "War of eighteen-twelve. God knows what kind of stuff is buried here. Artillery shells, shrapnel, bodies, evidently."

I didn't think the bones looked *that* old but I was in no mood to argue.

"This town does have a lot of ghosts," said Linda. "We took one of those haunted tours and they told us stories about war widows who died broken-hearted, and one about a doctor who murdered his wife and crippled son and buried their bodies in the basement of what is now one of the most popular restaurants in town."

"Don't forget the Angel Inn," a lady from the group chimed in. "They're very proud of their ghost."

The neighbors joined together in a chorus of "Oh yeah"s.

Linda turned to me. "The story goes that during the war, Captain Colin Swayze was having a love affair with the innkeeper's daughter. When an American victory looked inevitable, he went into the cellar to empty all the barrels of rum so the Americans wouldn't be able to celebrate. But he didn't get out of the cellar in time and hid in one of the barrels to avoid being captured. Apparently, the Americans went into the cellar, stabbing everything and anything with their bayonets and well . . ."

"Ewww," a few members of the group exclaimed.

"Yep, there are all kinds of secrets buried in this town."

During Linda's history lesson I noticed Erna Weins was missing from the group. I looked toward her house and saw, through the kitchen window, that she was on the phone. When she noticed me looking, she gave a quick wave and drew the drapes.

That night, long after the crowd outside had dispersed and the police had left, I thought back to what Linda had said about there being a lot of ghosts in this town. Recalling the contents of Moustache's hole, I knew this was no long-buried fallen soldier or eternally grieving widow. These were bones from a much more recent past than the one where soldiers wielded muskets and embarrassed doctors killed their imperfect children. Linda Yellman had certainly been right about one thing. Small towns did have their secrets and I had a feeling Moustache had just uncovered a dark one.

CHAPTER 4

It took a day or two for the police to finish digging up my backyard.

By the end of the week, the curious passersby passed by a little more quickly and the house reclaimed its position as one of the many charming but otherwise unremarkable cottages that lined the street.

I had heard nothing further from either Detective Sergeant Jeffers or Detective Staff Sergeant Raines. I was a bit sorry about the former, not so much about the latter. The neighbors had all moved their interests elsewhere. Even the reporter who interviewed me for the *Niagara Advance,* a local weekend newspaper, chose to focus on my time on *Port Authority* and my upcoming Shaw debut rather than the story he had been sent to cover.

I couldn't understand why the investigation seemed to have stopped almost as soon as it started and why the citizens of this small town seemed perfectly satisfied to chalk it up to a mere misfortune of the past and be done with it.

I knew Niagara-on-the-Lake was a popular destination for tourists from all over the world and had long enjoyed the reputation of being one of the prettiest towns in Canada, so I guess I could understand the desire to keep anything remotely sordid out of the news, but a part of me felt the bones in my backyard deserved more attention than they were getting. I couldn't shake the feeling that the bones had not, in fact, been resting in peace but had a story to tell.

For the time being, however, there was a different story that needed my attention, *Major Barbara*—the "flagship" show, the production that would open the Festival.

The Shaw Festival is comprised of three different theatres, each running four different productions in repertory. The Festival Theatre, home to the flagship production and usually a large scale musical in addition to two others, is the largest of the three, followed in size by the Royal George Theatre, originally an old vaudeville house, complete with red walls, gilded edges, and gold lions, and the smallest of the three, the Court House Theatre. Recently, the festival had added a fourth space called the Studio Theatre, which showcased plays that were outside the confines of the Festival's mandate to produce only pieces written by George Bernard Shaw and his contemporaries.

I, like most actors at the Shaw Festival, was contracted for two productions. The second of my shows, Harold Pinter's *The Hothouse*, was being performed in the studio space and didn't start rehearsing until mid-May.

Working in film and TV is very different from working in the theatre. Not every actor can make the transition. I hadn't even had one rehearsal yet and already my critics were casting doubt on my ability. Despite the fact that my resume listed numerous credits from summer theatre festivals and Montreal's English-speaking theatres, the fact that I had earned some kind of celebrity on TV was enough for them to decide that I was stepping on toes and stealing roles from better deserving actresses who had paid their theatrical dues.

I had moved to town several days before the start of rehearsals with the intention of preparing for my role as the title character but every time I tried to give one hundred percent to *Major Barbara*, my mind wandered to the bones. Before long I had more theories about them than Shaw had plays. In the end, I found myself cramming the night before the first rehearsal. Needless to say, "cranky" couldn't even begin to describe my mood when my alarm sang out bright and early Monday morning.

"I should never have taken this contract," I whined to my agent, Dean.

"You always say that."

"This time is different."

I had been with Dean for over a decade and it had become a regular thing for me to call him on the first day of rehearsal. To lament. I sat amidst a mountain of discarded clothes, hating absolutely everything I owned, knowing that my attire would be under as much critical fire as my acting.

"This time it's—"

"The same as all the other times, Bella. A roomful of artistic minds meeting for the first time, all with the same goal: to make magic."

"That's a load of crap and you know it. You know as well as I do that even though everyone tells you how great you were after the first reading, they all whisper about how much better they thought you'd be. Hell, I've done that. I know that's what goes on."

"Okay then, so what?"

"Dean!"

"Bella, all I'm saying is that everyone is in the same boat. You, the other actors, the designers, everyone. You all put pressure on yourselves to be perfect on the first day and, like it or not, you're not going to be. But that doesn't mean that the director is going to recast or the costume designers are going to throw out all their designs just because you may have put on a few pounds—"

"What?!"

"Not *you*. I'm talking generally." He paused and I took a moment to sulk. "Bella?"

"Yes?"

"If everyone was perfect on the first day, there would be no need for rehearsal. And if there was no rehearsal, there'd be fewer weeks on the contract which would mean less income for you and, more importantly, less income for *me*. Frankly, the more mediocre the better if we want to make any money in theatre."

I smiled. "Well, I'll do my best to be as mediocre as possible then. Heaven forbid you should starve on account of my brilliance."

I heard him chuckle. Dean had made a hefty commission off of me during my time on *Port Authority* and stood to make a pretty penny off my current contract as well. That was probably one of the reasons he continued to talk me off the ledge during my jittery, first-day-of-rehearsal phone calls.

I arrived at rehearsal to find that I was, in fact, not the centre of attention as I had presumed. That honor went to Olivia Childries, Canadian theatre royalty and a thirty-some-year veteran of the Festival, who had recently announced that this season would be her last.

"Oh, my God, isn't she fabulous! When I was seven I used to dress up in my mother's gowns and act out scenes from *Medea*." A whispering man, holding his chest with one hand and fanning himself with the other, quickly filled the chair beside me.

"How on earth did you know about *Medea* when you were seven? When I was seven I watched *Polka Dot Door* and the *Smurfs*, not a mother murdering her children."

"My mother was a slave to Public Broadcasting," the man offered, laughing. "One day while I was home sick with the chicken pox, they aired an Olivia Childries marathon. I an-

25

nounced to my mother, right then and there, that I wanted to be an actress! No need to come out after that, eh?" More laughing. It was infectious. "When I was offered this show, I just about died. I've been at the Festival for three seasons and every time I'm near her I practically hyperventilate. I've never spoken to her without falling all over myself and looking a complete ass. I can't believe I'm actually playing her son. Oh, I'm Adam, by the way. Adam Lange."

"Bella James," I said, enjoying him as much as he was enjoying Olivia.

"Oh, and don't worry, I think you're fabulous, too—"

"But you never quite get over your first love," I finished for him.

"You said it, sister!"

Olivia Childries was standing near the entrance of the rehearsal hall in conversation with Roberta Hayward, the Festival's artistic director and the director of this particular production. Everything about her seemed perfect—from her pixie haircut to the crease in her black slacks. Even her boots looked as if they had walked a clear path to the theatre, missing all of the slush and dirt that are inevitable in a spring thaw. Her white turtleneck sweater brought out the auburn highlights in her hair, despite the charcoal grey wool wrap that enveloped her slender frame. A pair of glasses that hung from a thin chain around her neck and an emerald ring set in gold and flanked by pearls were her only accessories. Those who knew her demonstrated some kind of familiarity, whether it was a kiss on the cheek, a full-on hug, or a gentle squeeze of the shoulder. Watching this display, it became clear that it was not only Adam who was enamored with her.

Much of the press surrounding the Festival centered on Olivia's impending departure from the stage and the theatre that had made her an icon. Somehow, Roberta Hayward and the board of directors came up with the idea that it would be fitting for Olivia to exit the festival in the same way she had debuted. So her final appearance would be as the well-mannered yet appallingly outspoken Lady Britomart Undershaft in the play that had made her a star some thirty-odd years before, when she played Barbara. That role now fell to me and with it a pressure I hadn't before considered. I watched Olivia Childries from my seat and realized, for the first time, the enormity of the task before me.

Adding to the mounting pressure I felt, I became increasingly aware of the extraordinarily large number of people milling about the rehearsal hall.

"Who are all these people?" I whispered to Adam, interrupting his conversation with the man on his other side.

"Invited guests."

"What do you mean 'invited guests'? They invite people to a first rehearsal?"

"Just the read through. They'll be gone this afternoon."

"Are you kidding me? What happened to 'This isn't a performance, it's simply a chance to hear the play out loud for the first time'?"

"They're members of the Shaw Guild, docents of the festival, other directors and designers. Don't be nervous, darling. Remember: you're fabulous." He winked.

"Don't be nervous says he who can't even look at Olivia Childries without fainting. Good luck with the opening scene."

"Oh, you bitch." He punctuated his mild oath with a playful slap on the arm.

Major Barbara begins with a lengthy dialogue between Lady Britomart and her son, Stephen. After quick, around-the-table introductions, we began to read. Anyone not noticing the iron grip Adam had on my left knee would never have guessed he was nervous. His usual open flamboyance gave way to the unfalteringly moral and gravely correct Stephen, and he held his own against the divine Olivia to such a degree that even she could not help being impressed.

At the intermission point, the stage manager called a fifteen-minute break and the group dissembled. Some excused themselves to use the washroom, a few made a mad dash for the door, no doubt to fill their lungs with as much nicotine as possible, but most people stayed to take advantage of the cookies and coffee that had been put together by some of the members of the Shaw Guild. I was fumbling with the milk carton when I felt a hand on my shoulder. I turned to find Olivia Childries smiling, dazzlingly, at me.

"Bella, it's a pleasure to meet you. I'm a big fan."

"Thank you. And likewise," I said, returning the smile and offering my hand.

She was focused so intently on me, like I was the only other person in the room. "When I heard you were going to be playing Barbara, I was absolutely thrilled. I couldn't imagine a better fit. We are going to have such fun, I think."

She had a slightly affected way of speaking. I've noticed a lot of actors have the tendency to "Britify" their speech somewhat. Not a full-on British accent—because they could never get away with that—but a slight elongation of vowels and added attention to enunciation. I didn't know what the desired effect of this was, but given that so many actors of the classical theatre adopted such behavior, I chalked it up to one of many things I would never fully understand.

"Ms. Childries, it's such an honor to be working with you, although, from what I gather, I have pretty big shoes to fill." While her eyes were smiling, she seemed to be searching for my meaning. "Your Barbara was quite definitive, I've heard."

"Oh, please, call me Olivia, and don't be silly. 'My Barbara,' as you say, was too many years ago to count. Many actresses have played the role here since and much better, too, I daresay. I have no doubt you'll do the same."

Of course, I didn't believe that any of her successors ever came close to matching her performance, and I was sure she didn't believe it either, but her self-deprecation was charming and I couldn't help but be completely won over by her.

"Now, my dear, I understand you had some excitement out your way," she said, changing the subject. "What was it, a body or something?"

"Not a body, per se, just bones. Looked like they'd been there quite a while. I haven't heard anything since the police left. I imagine they're in the process of trying to identify them but . . ."

"Oh, how horrible. What a shock that must have been. And the police have no ideas?"

"Not that I know of. But I'm not exactly on the 'need to know' list."

"Well, the whole thing is just awful," she said. "We certainly don't hear about that kind of thing around here very often. We're very lucky. Despite the start you've had to your time here, I think you'll find this little town to be quite wonderful. I can't imagine living anywhere else."

The stage manager called us back. Olivia gave my hand an affectionate squeeze before gliding back to her chair while I, far less gracefully, settled back into mine. She was exquisite and I knew, without a doubt, I had fallen under the same spell as Adam had when he was a mere seven years old.

CHAPTER 5

Excited by the day's creative energy, enchanted by Olivia Childries, and still somewhat troubled by the unidentified bones, I found myself staring at the ceiling in the wee hours of Tuesday morning. Reaching for my laptop I began surfing the web for information on my new, non-sexual, female crush.

I skimmed through umpteen reviews in which Olivia Childries was praised as being "divinely radiant" and "demanding all eyes" and "creating pure magic," before stumbling on a bit of her biographical trivia: born in Coldwater, Ontario, in 1951; father, a dentist, mother, a school teacher; married Mallard "Duck" Worthy in 1970, divorced in 1983—no children; married Peter Wynn in 1984, divorced in 2002—no children. The rest of the information detailed highlights from her lengthy theatrical career, which included most of the biggest theatres in the country.

Considering what a Canadian darling she was, I was surprised there wasn't more personal dirt, although I did find the quick turnaround from one marriage to the next to be somewhat intriguing. Mind you, her second husband, Peter Wynn, had been and still was Olivia's agent. By all accounts their wedding guests had comprised the who's who of Canadian theatre. At one time he had been considered the best in the biz, so I supposed it was only a matter of time before Canada's "it" girl and the man who helped get her the title found their way to each other.

I'd had the opportunity to meet Mr. Wynn on a couple of occasions and, while not altogether unpleasant, they were experiences I could have done without. This was a man who was always in the game and always looking to win, regardless of whom he took down along the way.

I could feel my eyes growing heavy at last and was about to shut my computer down when I came upon an article dated August 17, 1982:

SHAW ARTISTIC DIRECTOR BUYS HOUSE
OF HORROR
BY ANTON WILMS

In a shocking move, the Shaw Festival's Artistic Director, Phillip Southam, has opted to purchase the house in which one of the company's actresses was brutally attacked earlier this month. Residents of the town have been clamoring for the house's demolition since word spread of the vicious beating of rising star Olivia Childries, 31.

Southam defends his decision to buy the house: "It is out of love and support for Ms. Childries and her husband that I have chosen to purchase the house immediately. With today's market being what it is, there's no telling how long it would take to sell and I believe the sooner the house is out of their lives, the sooner they will be able to begin the healing process. My prayers are with them both during this extremely difficult time." Childries and her husband, a set builder for the theatre, purchased the house late last year after they both accepted invitations to come to the Festival.

Olivia Childries' portrayal of the title role in this season's *Major Barbara* has been deemed one of the most riveting and hypnotizing performances by an actress since Veronica Walters took the Stratford Festival by storm with her portrayal of Juliet in 1973.

Ms. Childries was found savagely beaten in her home on the evening of August 3rd. Reports suggest her injuries are so extensive that reconstructive surgery and years of physical rehabilitation will be required. No charges have yet been laid and no explanation has been given as to what might have prompted such a violent act.

Out of respect for Ms. Childries, the Shaw Festival has cancelled its remaining performances of *Major Barbara*. No word yet on what Southam plans to do with the house, although it is speculated he will resell the property at his earliest convenience.

Included with the article was a small thumbnail photograph of the house in question. I clicked on it to enlarge the view and found myself staring at a much younger version of the house in which I now sat, wide awake.

"Don't you think it's odd that she didn't say anything?"
I was on the phone with Natalie MacMahon, my best friend since university and the only person in the world whom I ever loved enough to shed my protective outer shell and show my true self in all its damaged glory.
"Maybe she doesn't know where you live," Natalie said.
"She knew about the bones," I countered.
"Just because she knew bones were discovered in your yard doesn't mean she knows where your yard is. Besides, even if she

did know, I'm sure the last thing she'd want to talk about with a complete stranger is the fact that you're living in the same house she was almost killed in thirty years ago."

"Yeah, I guess."

"Or maybe she does know and didn't want to frighten you. What's going on with those bones anyway?"

"I've no idea."

"You should call that detective. The cute one."

I had made the mistake of telling Natalie about Andre Jeffers.

"And say what?" I asked.

I knew where this was going. For years Natalie had been try-ing to fix me up with one guy or another, convinced that once I found love, I'd be able to let go of the demons of my past and live happily ever after. I was perfectly content, however, to live vicariously through her and her husband, Zack.

"Just inquire about how the investigation is coming along," she continued. "It's not like you don't have the right to ask. You did discover the body, after all. And then maybe the conversa-tion will turn to other things and—"

"Natalie."

"I'm just saying."

"I know what you're saying, thank you very much."

"Well, you have to admit Bel, left to your own devices—"

"Never mind."

It's not like I didn't date at all. I dated my *Port Authority* co-star, Rich Arborall, for five years. What started as a casual thing ended up being great publicity for the show, so we kept it going for as long as we could stand. After Rich, I had humored Nat-alie by going out with a few of her choice picks, none of whom had resulted in the next great Canadian romance, much to her dismay and my relief.

"I still think you should call him," she said, refusing to give up. "Besides, aren't you curious? Listen, why don't I come down for the night? We can call him together. Zack has a showing at a gallery tonight and Austin's been so squirrelly lately, getting out of the city will do him good."

Natalie and her husband lived in Toronto's granola west end. She was one of the top singing teachers in the industry and worked out of their home, while Zack, an artist, was the city's newest find and was in the enviable position of having works commissioned faster than he could keep up with. Austin was their Bernese mountain dog. One hundred and ten pounds of suck. Although he quadrupled Moustache in size, Austin had long played Charlie Brown to Moustache's Lucy.

"I rehearse 'til six," I said.

I knew with or without her there, she would not let up until I called Detective Sergeant Jeffers. Might as well have some company while I did so.

"Chinese?"

"Great."

The only thing I missed about Toronto was the food. No matter what you're craving, no matter what obscure ethnic delicacy, it could be found within blocks of anywhere. Chinatown was a veritable Shangri-la and, much to my delight, a little piece of it had come to Niagara-on-the-Lake in the back of Natalie's Honda Accord.

"Traffic was terrible," Natalie lamented, handing me one wonderfully smelling white plastic bag after another.

Austin was lifting his leg against the neighbor's hedge while Moustache stood, staring out from behind the screen door, his magnificent plume of tail down, head cocked to the right, brows furrowed. I could tell there was a growl brewing in his belly.

"So this is the 'house of horror,' eh?" Natalie said as she stood surveying the house with her overnight bag slung over one shoulder and Austin's bed tucked under the opposite arm.

"Shut up," I said and ushered her inside.

Moustache jumped up on Natalie, tail wagging, before snapping a warning at Austin, who was straddling the threshold, unsure of whether he should come in or not. I issued my own warning to Moustache, then proceeded to fawn over the Bernese, cradling his huge head in my hands and patting his muscular girth. Moustache voiced some jealousy, but finally resigned himself to the company and hurried to the kitchen, undoubtedly to make sure there was nothing in his dish for his guest to sample.

After a grand tour of the cottage and a visit to the backyard gravesite, Natalie and I plopped ourselves down in the living room with a bottle of red wine and the Chinese smorgasbord. Moustache sat on "his" chair, one eye on the food, the other on Austin, who was lying like a starfish on the floor. My search through the zillions of Styrofoam containers that held our feast finally yielded the dumplings and I readied my chopsticks to pierce one of the plump, pork-filled pillows.

"Not so fast." Natalie's hand swooped in and snapped the lid of the container down on my descending utensils. "Don't you have a phone call to make?"

"Are you serious? You're going to hold my dumplings hostage?"

She knew they were my favorite. Natalie picked up the container and proceeded to make a grand show of biting into a dumpling herself and moaning in delicious delight.

"Fine," I said, retrieving my cell phone from the kitchen and pulling Detective Jeffers' card out from behind the magnet that secured it to the fridge. I fired a faux glare in her direction before dialing. Relieved to get his voicemail, I left my name and number, told him I was curious about the investigation and asked him to call me at his convenience. Then I rescued my precious dumplings from Natalie's evil grasp and plopped two of them into my bowl with great flourish.

Feast fully underway, I deflected a few more jabs about my love life before Natalie launched into another one of my favorite subjects: my grandmother.

"How's Terri-Mae?"

"I haven't spoken to her since I moved."

"Bella!"

"I'll call! It's only been a week and, quite frankly, I think bodies appearing in my backyard is reason enough for . . . some . . ." I was scrambling and Natalie knew it. "I'll call her tomorrow."

My grandmother had the great misfortune of inheriting me after my parents were killed in a car accident. Losing my parents and being shipped across the country to Prince Edward Island to live with a woman with whom I'd only shared a handful of visits made me a real treat of an eight year old. Sullen, withdrawn, numb, I rejected every show of affection, every utterance of love, every kindness my grandmother bestowed upon me. Instead, I blamed her. I blamed her, the East Coast, the ocean, anything and everything for my misery. I left the day after my eighteenth birthday and met Natalie in Montreal a couple of years later.

After a night of drinking, I shared my story. In a moment of drunken clarity, I saw how my woe-is-me selfishness had obscured all compassion. Here was a woman who, because of me, was reminded daily of the son she had lost, and yet she buried her grief in an effort to ease mine. She changed her entire life to raise me the way she knew my parents would have wanted. The realization had hit me like a ton of bricks, as did the nausea from over-imbibing. Much of my anger and the "it's not fair" attitude I had held on to for over a decade were flushed down the toilet along with most of what I had consumed throughout that evening.

At Natalie's insistence, I had called Terri-Mae the next day and still, at Natalie's insistence, continued to do so every Sunday. Although many of my defenses are still intact, I knew our Sunday conversations were one of the highlights of Terri-Mae's week, even if she was the one forced to do most of the talking.

"I'll call her tomorrow," I repeated.

"You better," she said and flicked a snow pea in my direction.

All kidding aside, we both knew there was a lot of truth in what Natalie said. I kept people at a distance. I had a lot of "friends" but only one real *friend*. Natalie had been relentless at chipping away at my protective shell until there was enough space for her to wriggle herself in and see my elusive gooey center. We'd been friends for almost fourteen years and I often felt Natalie had saved my life.

I was helping myself to some Fu-Kien rice when the phone rang. My call display announced Andre Jeffers, to which Natalie responded with a squeal and "we need more wine." I answered while Natalie poured.

"Nice to hear from you, Detective Samuel." Jeffers' voice rang out on speakerphone.

I laughed. Natalie mouthed a "how cute" to which I mouthed a "shut up."

"So . . . curiosity is getting the better of you?"

"As a matter of fact, I haven't heard any news about the investigation and I was wondering how it was all going."

"Haven't got too much to report. Everything I know is what was discussed at the crime scene. If it is a crime scene. No obvious cause of death. It will probably take a little while yet to I.D. the bones. They're pretty old, as it turns out. Been in the ground thirty years, give or take. Coroner says they're female, but that's about it. We won't know anything further without running more tests. He said he'd try to match DNA to some of our missing persons before sending the bones to Hamilton for a Forensic Pathologist to look at, but thinks that's a dead end as none of our MPs date that far back. Other than that, your guess is as good as mine. Raines took over the case and is keeping pretty closed-mouthed about it."

That explained why there had been nothing in the news.

"I shouldn't be telling you all this," he added.

"Don't worry, I won't say anything," I said and shot a warning look to Natalie, who was listening intently.

"Not that there's much to say anyway," he said, disappointed.

"I'm sorry. I know you really wanted a chance to impress Raines."

"It's not that I want to, I *need* to. My probation period is up in June. If I don't do something worthy, I could end up back at B.E.U."

"B.E.U.?"

"Biker Enforcement Unit."

"Really?"

I couldn't picture the somewhat vertically challenged Jeffers, with his GQ-mussed hair, taking on a Hell's Angel twice his size.

"Don't I look the type?" he joked. The chuckle that had accompanied my declaration of disbelief had obviously tipped him off to the cartoon that was playing out in my mind. I fumbled for something to say, but he mercifully let me off the hook. "Three years in B.E.U. I loved it but my wife cried every time I left to go to work. Terrified the gangs would come looking for revenge or something. When we decided to start a family, she made me promise to find a job in another department, so when an opening came up in Major Crimes I jumped at it."

Following the mention of his wife, any further details barely registered. Natalie's jaw fell open, her head fell back, and she dismissed the phone with a wave of her hand before moving toward the kitchen to retrieve another bottle of wine. I simply shook my head, humiliated that I had let Natalie drag me in to her little fantasy. Jeffers was still talking.

". . . little boy due in July so I'm at the mercy of Raines."

"Any way you could conduct your own investigation?" I asked.

"This isn't TV. I can't start poking around behind his back."

Natalie returned with more wine and was gesturing me to wrap it up. I brushed her off. Married or not, I liked Andre Jeffers and I felt badly for him. He was talking again, but I wasn't listening. My wheels were turning and I quickly interrupted.

"Wait a minute. How long did you say those bones had been there?"

"Thirty years, give or take. But that was a preliminary estimate."

"Would it help if I told you who was living in this house thirty years ago?"

"How would you know something like that?"

I told Jeffers about the article I had found and emailed him the link, unsure of whether I wanted something to come of it or not.

CHAPTER 6

Rehearsal the next morning was proving to be more frustrating than fruitful. I hadn't slept well the night before—a combination of too much wine, girl talk, and a newly piqued curiosity about the investigation (or non-investigation).

Additionally, I was struggling with my last scene in which Barbara comes to the realization that mankind cannot be saved by the Bible alone and must accept that, in order for good to exist in the world, so too must the bad and that, often, the two make unlikely bedfellows. Not that I was one to argue with Shaw, but I felt that Barbara's transfiguration—Shaw's word— happened too quickly and I was failing in my efforts to make the moment make sense.

As a topper, Jarod Riley, the actor playing my fiancé, was one of those method types who felt since our characters were in love, we should give it a try. He was a lovely man and an excellent actor, but our ideas about fraternization were very different. I spent every break avoiding his gaze and rejecting his suggestions of grabbing dinner.

We broke for lunch at one o'clock and by pulling a container of Chinese leftovers out of my bag I dashed Jarod's hopes of joining me for lunch in the greenroom, a lounge area for members of the company. Adam and Olivia sidled by me, arm-in-arm, and caught the tail end of my rejection.

"Can't blame a guy for trying," Adam teased. "I'm off in search of some romance of my own. The guy playing Dick

Dudgeon in *The Devil's Disciple* is gorgeous!" he announced, singing the last word. "I'm going to 'accidentally' bump into him outside Rehearsal Hall three." He winked before leaving the room.

"I hope he has more luck than Jarod is having," I said to Olivia.

"Ah, the showmance. Jarod will get over it eventually," she said, obviously speaking from experience.

"Yeah, when his next show starts and he has a new leading lady."

We both laughed.

"I thought you were dating that delicious looking man from your show," Olivia remarked, catching me a bit off guard.

"Talk about your showmances," I managed to get out.

Had she been doing some cyber stalking? Or had she happened upon a back issue of one of those magazines that pride themselves on celebrity gossip? I was leaning toward the stalking as I had done some "research" of my own.

I decided two could play this game and asked, nonchalantly, "What about you?"

"Dating? No. I like my independence."

"But you were married."

"Almost twenty years. My agent. Can't get more showmance than that, can you?"

She chuckled and I smiled in solidarity. I found it odd she made no mention of her first marriage. Based on the timeline I had discovered, the quick turnaround into marriage number two implied that there might have been something on the side, but I still felt twelve years was too long a time to spend with someone without it warranting a mention. Wondering if it was her first husband who beat her up, I decided to give the envelope a little nudge.

"Twenty years! Wow! Ever think about getting married again

41

or was once enough?"

Olivia's eyes flashed for a moment before her face settled back into its calm façade. She laughed. So did I. We'd both been caught in our mutual curiosity of each other.

"I got married the first time when I was nineteen," she said. "My high school sweetheart. That's what you did in those days. Got married soon after graduation, had kids, and became your parents. But both of us dreamed bigger than that and, after a while, we grew into different people. I have no regrets. He was a wonderful man and we did go into marriage with the best of intentions."

I didn't catch any trace of fear or animosity in her voice, which gave little credence to my theory of him being her attacker. In fact, I didn't catch much emotion at all. I chalked that up to the passage of time. Eventually, certain events take on a detached matter-of-factness.

Feeling the subject of her attack was best left for another day, if ever, I switched gears and mentioned the difficulty I was having with the last scene. I hoped she might impart some insight as to how she had played it decades prior, but I was out of luck. My inner self chuckled. No matter how much time passes, actors will never divulge their secrets for fear of having someone play a role better than they did.

Olivia's cell phone rang, and she excused herself to answer it. I took the opportunity to scoop some fried noodles into my mouth. I watched Olivia's face transform. It was as if she had walked into a shadow. She uttered something to me about having to get to the greenroom before there was nothing left for lunch, and rushed out. Her exit was almost perfect, except she resumed her phone conversation too soon on her way out of the rehearsal hall. I managed to catch, "What are you talking about? I'm afraid I don't think . . ." before she was out of earshot.

★ ★ ★ ★ ★

The rest of the day's rehearsal hovered between exasperating and maddening: Jarod Riley, none too cleverly, kept embellishing the kiss our characters shared at the end of the play, while Olivia was completely distracted and kept losing her focus, inciting the fury of the actor playing Andrew Undershaft. Adam was wallowing in petulance after his "run in" with Dick Dudgeon revealed the latter to be a "dick" indeed. When six o'clock mercifully came, *Major Barbara* was a virtual "Comedy of Errors."

I was invited to go for a drink by Adam and offered a ride home by Jarod. I declined on both fronts, wanting to get home to Moustache and the wonderful way he had of drowning out the rest of the world for me.

And if there was some word from Jeffers, that would be nice, too.

It was about a twenty-five minute walk from the theatre to my cottage and the brisk March evening was just what I needed to refuel my tank and let my mind wander. After thinking through Barbara's final monologue, I began to theorize about Olivia's mysterious phone call. I had already come up with four utterly fantastic scenarios when I rounded the corner to my street and saw Olivia making a quick exit from Erna Weins' robin's egg and an even quicker exit out of her driveway. Any hope she may have had of being inconspicuous vanished with the same speed at which her car took off up the street.

Focusing on Olivia's back end rather than where I was going, I, quite literally, bumped into the car sitting in my driveway.

"Hope you've got insurance, ma'am." Jeffers *tsked* and emerged from the car with a smirk.

"Hope you've got a good reason for trespassing," I countered.

"As a matter of fact—"

"Hang on. Did you happen to see that car that just peeled out of here?"

"Sure did. Driver had a heated exchange with the woman inside. Left in a hurry and the rest I'm sure you saw. Whole thing lasted about fifteen minutes. Why?"

"That was Olivia Childries," I whispered.

"And, let me guess, the woman in the house was Mrs. Erna Weins."

"How did you know that?"

"You got a minute?"

Moustache was trotting ahead of us, stretching the extend-o leash to its max, savoring every sniff and relishing in each lift of his leg. Jeffers was telling me about how he'd decided to do a little covert investigating after all and how he'd managed to get his hands on some of the files on Olivia's attack.

"Sloppy police work, as far as I can see. A couple of things don't add up. According to the report, Olivia's attack occurred on the evening of Tuesday, August 3, 1982. A neighbor called in a disturbance a little after eight p.m. and officers responded about twenty minutes after that."

"Let me guess—Erna Weins was the good neighbor?"

"You got it! I called her earlier and she and I had a lovely chat. For an old woman she's got quite the memory. I asked her if she could recall any of the details about the night of Olivia's attack and she rattled off how she had heard Olivia pleading with someone to get out, how she heard her screaming and begging for them to stop. Said it sounded like things were being crashed into. Almost verbatim to what's in the file. Strange thing is, according to statements from other neighbors on the night in question, not only did no one see anything, but no one mentioned hearing anything."

"That's an awful lot of noise for no one else to hear."

"Great minds, Detective Samuel."

He seemed to delight in the company of my TV alter ego. I didn't mind. Frankly, Emma Samuel had more business sticking her nose in this than I did.

"Something else," he went on. "Mrs. Weins said she called the police as soon as she heard the crashes. However . . ." He paused for a moment to hand me some photos.

They were photos of the night Olivia was attacked. Blood spatter, Olivia's unconscious body. I came to a close-up of her face and had to cover my mouth with my hand. She was unrecognizable. If I didn't know better, I would doubt what I looked at was even human.

"You okay?" Jeffers asked. I nodded and swallowed hard. "I'm sorry. I should have warned you."

"How could somebody do something like that to another person?"

Jeffers gave me a minute before continuing his story. "Anyway, when I showed these pictures to a friend of mine in the coroner's office, he said there's no way twenty minutes would have been enough time for bruising of this extent to form. Said he couldn't put a definite timeline on it without seeing the victim in person, but he felt pretty sure the bruising in these photographs is consistent with at least an hour's passing. If Mrs. Weins called when she said she did and the police arrived twenty or so minutes later, there's another forty minutes to account for."

"You think she lied about when she called it in?"

"I don't know. But that's not all. Report states that as soon as Olivia Childries regained consciousness, she demanded the investigation be dropped immediately. Refused to give any description whatsoever of the person who attacked her. Said the whole thing was too traumatic and she didn't want to have to relive any part of it. Case was closed as quickly as it was opened."

"And the department went along with that?"

"Victim's rights."

"That doesn't make any sense. If I were Olivia, I'd be terrified whoever did it would come back to finish the job."

"Unless she knew her attacker and was trying to protect him."

I found that hard to believe but, sadly, not impossible. We walked for a bit in silence.

A thought struck me. "What time did you say you talked to Erna Weins?"

"Must have been a little after one, I think."

I told Jeffers about the call Olivia had received around that time and how she'd left me so abruptly. If Erna had called her after speaking with Jeffers to tell her the police were asking questions about that night, it would definitely account for the mood she was in for the rest of the afternoon and her post-rehearsal visit. What it didn't explain was her anger toward Erna.

Jeffers agreed that Erna calling Olivia seemed to fit the bill and promised to check the phone records.

"Did Erna say anything else?" I asked, hopeful.

"Nothing we didn't already know."

"What's going on? Thirty years ago, a woman is brutally beaten in the same house where, thirty years later, another woman's body is discovered. And nobody wants to talk about either incident. There's got to be a connection!"

He merely shrugged. My mind was reeling.

"What about her first husband? Did anyone talk to him that night?"

I filled Jeffers in about the divorce that took place not long after the attack and the quickie marriage that followed.

"Makes sense. Wife has an affair, husband flies into a jealous rage, wife doesn't press charges because she feels guilty, quick divorce, and the whole thing is water under the bridge. That wouldn't explain the bones that were uncovered, but, hey, one puzzle at a time." He took a moment to double-check the pages in his hand. "These say the husband showed up at the house shortly after nine p.m. Had a towel around his right hand. The officer told him what had happened and the husband left immediately for the hospital. Other than that exchange, he was never interviewed."

"Are you kidding me? The husband is always the prime suspect in cases like these. Initially, anyway. Even the worst Hollywood cop drama would get that right. Who was the idiot cop in charge of this case?"

"Funny you should ask," said Jeffers handing over a file folder.

"Skip Raines?"

I was more convinced than ever that there was a connection between the two cases. Jeffers himself had questioned why Raines was on the scene when the bones were discovered and had raised an eyebrow again when he took over the investigation. A Staff Sergeant is usually too busy running the unit to worry about doing fieldwork. Raines obviously recognized the address when I called in about the bones. Either he was a better detective than I was giving him credit for or . . . I didn't know how to finish that thought, but I *did* know I was not about to start handing out ribbons of merit.

"The one person who could actually shed some light on this whole thing—"

"I know," Jeffers cut in.

We had arrived back at my house. Moustache sat patiently by the front door, staring at it as if willing it to open.

"So what are you going to do?" I asked.

"Something that should have been done years ago. Talk to the husband."

"You really want to keep going with this? You said Raines has taken complete control of the case. If he finds out you've been investigating without his authority—"

"Oh, I'm well aware of what will happen if Raines finds out."

"And you're willing to take the risk?" I was impressed.

Jeffers shrugged. "What's the worst that can happen? I get sent back to B.E.U."

"You could get kicked off the force," I corrected.

For a moment we just stared at one another. He was well aware of the consequences, I could see that.

"What changed your mind?" I asked. "When I suggested conducting your own investigation before, it was out of the question."

He took a moment before answering. "You ever argue with a pregnant woman?"

I knew Jeffers was making a joke to lighten the seriousness of what he was suggesting. I guessed his desire to put his career on the line stemmed more from the fact that he was a good cop who, true to his oath, wanted to see the right thing done and a poor woman laid to rest where she belonged. I also figured he knew his time in Major Crimes was limited. Raines was never going to cut him a break and, without one, he'd never have the chance to prove his worth. It was too bad. The world could use more cops like Jeffers.

"You're going to be a great dad," I said, admiring his conviction and wishing I'd had such a role model in my own life.

He smiled, lowering his eyes. I detected a bit of remorse in his decision but not enough for him to reconsider.

"Hey, you hungry? I've got a fridge full of Chinese leftovers."

"No, thanks." Jeffers walked to the driver's side of his car. "I'm off in search of a seafood enchilada with a side of fries and French onion dip." Reacting to the look on my face, he said, "I asked before—you ever argue with a pregnant woman?"

I laughed and went to join Moustache who was still staring at the door, hoping for some sort of divine intervention.

"So how's Sunday?" Jeffers asked over the roof of the car.

"For what?"

"Road trip. Husband's in Coldwater."

"You want me to go with you?"

"Every good detective has a partner and this was your idea, Samuel."

"Jeffers, Emma Samuel is not a real detective!"

"Bella," he started and I could sense a hint of desperation, "you are the only other person who has taken any interest in this case. Raines isn't going to let me anywhere near this and there are things he's missing, you said it yourself. It's not like I want you to pretend you're a police officer. I just want another set of eyes and ears, that's all." I hesitated. "I'm already taking a chance by looking into this case. Including you as my 'partner' will be the least of my misdemeanors."

"Oh, I don't know about that," I said. "I think there are pretty strong consequences for involving civilians."

"Maybe," he said with a twinkle in his eye. "But if we find something useful, I'm hoping it won't matter so much."

I smiled in spite of every instinct telling me this was a bad idea. "Okay."

"Great! I'll pick you up at eight. I'll supply the coffee, you supply the breakfast." He rolled down the passenger side window and added, "No donuts. I'm trying to cut out the sugar."

"I drink tea," I yelled after him as he was pulling away. "Green!"

Jeffers honked in response and drove off in culinary pursuit.

I shook my head and muttered to Moustache about what I had just gotten myself roped in to when I noticed the drapes in Erna Weins' kitchen swaying slightly. I wondered if she had been watching me, but then the cream-colored cat jumped onto the windowsill, disturbing the drapes further. I imagined the cat probably spent much of its day engaged in this kind of neighbor-hood watch and I laughed at my paranoia.

CHAPTER 7

Sunday morning brought Jeffers, as promised. While he was morning glory personified, I was already looking for my second wind as my first wind had gone back to bed.

"Howdy, Pardner," Jeffers drawled as I folded myself into the passenger seat of his Jetta.

He handed me an orange travel mug filled with hot water and a tea bag.

"You got off easy," I said taking the mug and giving a breakfast burrito in return.

"A feast, Samuel! You shouldn't have," he said before folding back the waxed paper and taking a bite.

An eye roll from me. "As if you gave me a choice."

Jeffers chewed a smile in my direction. "By the way, your neighbor's watching us," he said, nonchalantly, looking in his rearview mirror as he backed out of the driveway.

"How do you know?" I turned awkwardly in my seat to get a better view of Erna Weins' kitchen window. I saw nothing that would suggest spying eyes.

"A trained eye, Samuel."

I was still staring at the house as we drove away, disappointed that nothing, in my seven years of playing a master detective, had rubbed off in real life. Maybe the paranoia I'd so easily dismissed a few days before had been real. I couldn't understand what Erna hoped to gain by watching me. There was no way she could know what Jeffers and I were up to. And I was fairly certain she had no idea the man in the car with me was the same man with whom she'd had a phone conversation earlier in the week. As far as Erna knew, my involvement with the bones ended when the police tape around my house came down, and there was nothing to tie me to the renewed interest in Olivia's attack. So what was she looking for? Was she looking at all? I was beginning to think my engaging in a rogue assignment with Jeffers was making me jump at shadows that didn't exist.

It was a two-and-a-half-hour drive northeast to Coldwater. Jeffers and I used that time to prep our cover story. We'd have to be as inconspicuous as possible. Hard to do when asking questions that should have been asked thirty years ago about a case that was only open for a minute and a half and which was possibly linked to the bones of a young woman whom nobody seemed to miss. Jeffers had done some digging and learned that a string of recent break-ins had rocked Coldwater's small community, including one at the furniture store that the ex-husband in question owned and operated. We decided taking this angle would be our way in. Jeffers and I would pose as police officers from a neighboring town, investigating a possible link between the robberies in Coldwater and some suspicious events in "our" jurisdiction.

"Once we're in," said Jeffers, "I can easily steer the conversation to the night of Olivia's attack."

"As simple as that?"

"I'm a master detective, Samuel. Watch and learn."

It took three knocks and a muffled "Just a minute" before the door was finally answered.

"Can I help you?" a woman in her sixties asked from behind the screen door.

The smell of rhubarb hung in the air around her and slowly wafted through the door to reach Jeffers and me on the porch.

"Mrs. Worthy?" Jeffers asked.

"Yes."

"Sorry to bother you, ma'am," said Jeffers, flashing his badge. "We're hoping to have a few words with your husband. Is he around?"

I noticed that Jeffers had not introduced himself or me by name.

"Nothing serious, ma'am," Jeffers continued, putting her at obvious ease. "Just wanted to ask a few questions about the string of robberies in the area."

"Oh, of course," she said with a smile. "He's out back in his workshop. Come, I'll show you." She joined us on the porch. "Please excuse my appearance," she said, indicating the flour-spattered apron that hung over her clothes and the oven mitts she was in the hasty process of removing. "Getting pies ready for the Spring Fair. We're expecting an even bigger turnout than last year."

Jeffers listened intently as Mrs. Worthy rattled on about Spring Fairs past and the important role her pies played in their success. He made Mrs. Worthy his sole focus during this brief walk to the back of the house, and it was quite clear she enjoyed the attention. Her sparkling eyes and the way her hand kept moving up to primp her light brown hair were all telltale signs of a woman charmed. After such a display, I was surprised that she even remembered why we were there.

"Duck?" Mrs. Worthy called, peeking her head around the door of the large garage that had been converted to a wood-shop. The hum of some sort of saw underscored a muffled response. "There are some police here to ask you a few questions about the burglaries."

The saw made one more screech before whirring to a stop. Mrs. Worthy ushered us inside. The workshop smelled of freshly cut cedar and boasted evidence of Duck Worthy's artistry. Most of the pieces were unfinished: the frame of a dresser missing its drawers, a couple of chairs waiting for seats, an armoire that was short one of its doors. In the back corner of the shop were some finished pieces waiting to be transferred from their birthplace to Worthy's downtown store. Sawdust hung in the air, momentarily suspended in time, as if trying to decide which surface to land on.

Duck Worthy stood in the middle of this cloud. His size seemed to belie the delicate detailing that showed in his craftsmanship. He stood well over six feet and was built much like the armoire that stood against the rear wall, broad and solid. Although now nearly all white, Duck's full head of hair betrayed some of its original darkness and his skin showed none of the lines and wear of most people his age. He was movie-star handsome, made even more so by his obvious lack of awareness of this fact. I took a minute to envision him alongside Olivia and found myself smiling at the thought of how stunning they must have looked together. A quick glance at Mrs. Duck left me disappointed. While by no means unattractive, she lacked the striking presence both Olivia and Duck commanded, and I felt a momentary regret that, somehow, Duck Worthy had remarried well beneath his physical station.

"Don't know what I can tell you that hasn't already been told," Duck said, extending a large, rough hand to both Jeffers and me in welcome.

Mrs. Worthy quietly excused herself and returned, I guessed, to her pies.

"Anything at all you might remember. We've reason to believe whoever's behind the Coldwater robberies may have ventured further afield," said Jeffers, launching into our cover story.

"Everything I know is in the report. Didn't see the guys and haven't had any trouble since. Did hear the Millards up on Main recently had an attempt made on their place. Dogs got to barking and the guys fled. You may want to check in with them. They may be of more help, having had it just happen and all."

"Thank you, we will," said Jeffers, scribbling the information in his notebook. "Not every day Coldwater makes the crime news is it? Of course, every few years there's something that shakes up these parts." Duck Worthy's eyes narrowed but Jeffers continued. "A few years ago that poor girl was raped at the Fall Fair; then there was that fire that killed the entire Potts family in eighty-nine. Never did catch the creep who started that." Jeffers shot a quick glance in my direction and I knew he was about to introduce the guest of honor. I held my breath. "And who can forget that horrible attack on that actress, what was it, thirty-some years ago? Now granted, that didn't happen here, but she was from Coldwater, if I'm not mistaken. Made national news."

The light went out from behind Duck Worthy's eyes. "If there's nothing else," he said flatly and utterly emotionless, "I'd like to get back to work."

He fixed his dead stare on Jeffers, who held his ground. Our charade was done and it was time to get what we came for.

"Mr. Worthy, there have been some new findings that we think might be linked to Olivia Childries' attack," Jeffers said quickly. "If there is anything at all that you can tell us about that night it would be—"

"I'd like you to leave," Duck growled.

"Mr. Worthy, we know this is difficult but it would really be helpful if—"

The entrance of Mrs. Duck brought an end to Jeffers' appeal, and I saw his shoulders slump in surrender. Mrs. Worthy carried a tray on which lay three cups, a cozy covered teapot, and three pieces of steaming rhubarb pie. She wore her most dazzling smile and was muttering an apology to Jeffers for interrupting when Duck cut her flirtation short.

"Never mind, Shelagh. These folks were just leaving."

"Oh, but surely you have time for some pie," Shelagh Worthy said, her eyes twinkling at Jeffers. No acknowledgment of me whatsoever.

Jeffers met Duck's stare before turning to Shelagh and echoing her husband's sentiment.

"Well, just give me a minute and I'll pack it up for you," she cooed and turned to go.

"Leave it, Shelagh!"

She stood in the doorway of the workshop and looked from her husband to Jeffers and back again before the tension in the room settled upon her.

"I trust you can find your way," Duck Worthy said.

"Thank you very much for your time." Jeffers tipped his metaphorical hat to Mrs. Worthy and we submissively stepped into the bright sunlight.

Neither Jeffers nor I said much during the drive back to Niagara-on-the-Lake, but we did manage to share a few theories as to what had made Duck Worthy clam up at the mere mention of Olivia's name. Jeffers was sure Duck was the one responsible for her attack. I wasn't. He didn't have the air of a guilty man but rather a man broken. Like he had suffered something terrible that, contrary to his outer strength, he still carried deep inside. Regardless, we were no closer to finding out what happened to Olivia that night or how, even *if,* it related to the unidentified bones. I was beginning to think both cases were growing colder by the minute.

CHAPTER 8

It is a hateful thing when the phone rings before the alarm clock goes off. It is such a violation of the sanctity of sleep, especially when the sleep in question involves two and a half hours of staring at the ceiling. I threw the covers over my head, willing the ringing to stop and trying desperately to hold on to the few precious winks I had finally been able to salvage. No such luck.

Reaching my arm out of the warmth of my duvet, I fumbled around for the phone and mumbled something even I didn't understand into the receiver.

"Campbell?" said the female voice on the line.

I hesitated. I had been named after my paternal grandfather who passed away shortly before my birth. My parents had shortened the moniker to Bella and only ever used my full name whenever I was in trouble. "Campbell Vivienne James" had been uttered probably more times than my parents had wished. Now the only people who called me by my full given name were my grandmother and telemarketers.

"Campbell, it's Marie Coombs," she said, then paused to let the name register.

My breath caught. This wasn't going to be good news. "Of course, Marie. Is everything all right?" I asked, my voice faltering slightly.

Marie had been Terri-Mae's neighbor and dear friend for as long as I could remember and had been witness to many of my "shining" moments growing up. The only reason she would be calling me was if something had happened to Terri-Mae.

"I'm so sorry to call at such an hour."

"Not at all, Marie," I said, sensing the difficulty the woman was having on the other end of the line.

"Campbell, I'm so sorry."

I closed my eyes and took a few deep breaths to steady myself. After a few sobs, Marie began talking again but her words barely registered.

The day before had been Sunday and I hadn't called.

"The doctor said it was an aneurysm," I told Natalie over the phone. "Marie said Terri-Mae had complained of a headache earlier in the afternoon. They were having tea at the church and Terri-Mae decided to go home and sleep it off. When Marie stopped by to pick her up for their bridge game later that evening . . ." My voice trailed off to allow for the image of poor Marie discovering the lifeless body of her lifelong friend. After a deep breath I continued. "Marie had just returned home from the hospital and called me right away."

"Oh, Bella, I'm so sorry. Did Terri-Mae mention anything about a headache when you called her yesterday?"

"Um, no," I lied, too ashamed to admit, even to Natalie, that in my preoccupation with Olivia Childries and Duck Worthy, I had failed my grandmother yet again.

I was sure Natalie could sense my deceit and was grateful she didn't push the matter. She would know, of course, that the guilt I felt was far worse than any dressing down she could give me.

I spent the rest of the day in a kind of fog. Throughout rehearsal my mind view-mastered its way through old memories of Terri-Mae; made up images of what her final moments were like;

shuffled through soundtracks of conversations past and recent, and my morning exchange with Marie, who graciously offered to handle the funeral arrangements and oversee the sale of Terri-Mae's house. In my heart of hearts I knew Marie was far better suited than I to tend to Terri-Mae's affairs, but the realization of this sat upon my shoulders with a weight only Atlas himself could have withstood.

Adam picked up on my mood right away and after some gentle pressing on his part, I confided my plight. Not only did he prove to be a great comfort, he successfully kept Jarod Riley at least twenty feet away from me, and masterfully deflected any questions or comments about my emotional state. I had found another kindred spirit in Adam, but in my guilt over Terri-Mae and what had become of our relationship, I wasn't sure I deserved him.

To add insult to injury, our stage manager, Caitlin, a wisp of a woman, so tiny that even the weight of her glasses seemed to threaten her balance, informed me that the *Globe and Mail* newspaper would be arriving at five p.m. to conduct an interview with Olivia and me. She had a way of speaking that made it sound like she was apologizing for what she was saying. Having a conversation with her always exhausted me. I found myself coloring my side of the dialogue with as much re-assurance as possible in order to counter her self-recrimination.

I looked to where Olivia was sitting with her perfect makeup and perfect hair and flashed back to the last image I had of myself, this morning, in the bathroom mirror. Ponytail, tunic top and yoga pants did not a cover girl make. Unless, of course, it was for an issue of one of those gossip rags women shell out a fortune for in an effort to make themselves feel better by look-ing at pictures of celebrities sans makeup. This was Karma bit-ing me in the ass, plain and simple, and I deserved every nip and nibble.

★ ★ ★ ★ ★

I had forgotten my cell phone on the kitchen counter and could hear its ringing before I opened the door to my cottage. My shoulders slumped at the very thought of having to endure any more social interaction. I stood with my keys in my hand until the ringing stopped. I could hear Moustache snorting on the other side of the door. He'd obviously heard me climb the steps and was confused as to why I hadn't yet made an appearance.

I could picture him sitting, as he always did when he sensed my coming home, so he would be the first thing I'd see when I opened the door. I turned the key and pushed the door open and the picture in my mind's eye became a reality. With his whole body wagging, Moustache jumped up to lean against my legs while I nuzzled and squeezed and told him how I had missed him.

Our mutual adoration was interrupted by the phone. Again, I let it go, figuring whomever was calling would leave a message. Four rings and then silence. I looked at the message screen, waiting for the message notification to come on. It didn't and I didn't care.

Moustache took off at a gallop to stand by the sliding doors in the kitchen, waiting to be let out. I followed. With the dog happily making the rounds of the backyard, I moved to pour myself a glass of wine. More ringing. I snatched at the phone, checking the call display. Unknown number. Whoever was calling was relentless. I decided to get it over with.

"Hello?" I said, after taking a calming breath.

"Ms. James?" A woman's voice.

"May I ask who's calling?" A pause. "Hello?"

"This is Shelagh Worthy."

That got my attention.

"I'm sorry to bother you," she said. "I wanted to apologize for my husband. I'm afraid he was very rude to you and your

60

friend when you were out at the house yesterday."

"Not at all," I managed to say through my utter confusion.

"I recognized you from *Port Authority*. Never missed an episode."

"Well, thank you." I was taken aback by her admission as she had shown no signs of recognition the day before.

"Duck's a very private person and that time in his life is very difficult for him to talk about."

"Of course."

"The night Olivia was attacked was extremely painful for him. For all of us. I mean, Olivia was my best friend. She still is. But poor Duck's never gotten over it."

I got the feeling she had more to say and would be quite happy for this to be a one-sided conversation, so I let her have the floor.

"You see, Olivia was having an affair and Duck happened to walk in on her and . . . Peter. Duck never confronted them. He just left the house. A few hours later the attack occurred. Duck felt incredible guilt, kept saying that if he had stayed and hashed it out, maybe the attack wouldn't have happened. In spite of her betrayal, he loved Olivia very much."

Up until this point, Shelagh Worthy had been chattering away in a perfect balance of sympathy and straightforwardness.

"Duck had always loved Olivia," she continued, her tone changing. "Since we were all kids together." I detected a bitterness mixed with resentment, subtle but still undeniable. "The two of them were the perfect couple, you know. The couple everyone else wanted to be?"

This last statement was presented as a question, as if she was looking for validation.

I threw in an obligatory "Hmm," which seemed to appease and she carried on.

"I was with Olivia at the hospital and I was the one who had to tell Duck she didn't ever want to see him again. That she was moving on with Peter. And she was true to her word. She never saw Duck again." There was no trace of the bitterness I had detected earlier and I began to think I had imagined it.

"What do you mean she never saw him again? They never met after the attack? Not to finalize the divorce or anything?"

"Never. You have to understand, Olivia had been through so much trauma. She needed to get rid of all the negative things in her life and focus on the positive: healing and her life with Peter. And she certainly didn't want to set foot in that house again or have any reminders of it. Duck packed it all up, signed the papers, and gave her what she wanted."

"Mrs. Worthy," I began, carefully, "do you have any idea who may have attacked Olivia?"

She took a deep breath. "No."

"Mrs. Worthy—"

I heard what sounded like a car door slam but couldn't tell if the sound had come from Shelagh Worthy's end or closer to home.

"I'm sorry, Ms. James, Duck just got in. If he knows I'm talking to you about this he'll be furious. I tried calling earlier so we would have more time. I hope I've answered your questions."

"Mrs. Worthy, wait!"

My appeal was met with a dial tone. I slammed the phone down. Question after question sped across my brain like a news scroll on the bottom of a television screen. I had to talk to Jeffers. But first, I needed to gather my racing thoughts into some semblance of organization, otherwise I'd be wasting his time. I grabbed Moustache's leash from its hook by the front door and went to meet him out back, hoping a brisk walk around the neighborhood would do the trick.

"Moustache," I called, jingling his leash.

His walks were the highlight of his day and the mere sight of his leash in my hands was enough to send him into a fit of triple axels and mad tail-wagging. But this time, silence.

"Moustache?" I called again, as I descended the steps of the back deck.

Still nothing. I saw that the gate was open. My heart leapt into my throat. While Moustache was perfect in every other way, he was as curious as the monkey, George, and not at all car-wise. I ran through the gate calling his name, panic rising. No response. I was standing in the middle of the road looking up and down the street, not knowing which way to run, when I saw a flash of beige in a bush about six houses away.

"Moustache!" I cried.

He stuck his head out of the shrubbery and looked at me. I breathed a sigh of relief and started my approach. "Come here."

I shook his leash and tried to keep my voice calm so as not to upset him. His tail went into a wag and he started toward me. He had taken no more than three steps when he stumbled. He looked at me and, if it's possible for a dog to express confusion, he was doing so. I quickened my pace. He took a few more steps and stumbled again. I broke into a run and managed to reach him just in time for him to collapse in my arms.

CHAPTER 9

"He's awake."

The vet's voice sounded muffled inside the bubble of numbness I had been sitting in. I'd arrived at the animal hospital minutes after it had closed for the day, but my incessant banging on the door and the sight of the apparently lifeless dog in my arms had sent all hands into action without a moment's hesitation. I'm sure my sobbing might have had something to do with that, too. After many assurances that Moustache was in the best possible hands, the receptionist gave up trying to engage me in conversation and left me to vanish inside myself while I waited.

Just like I had waited before. Only when you're eight, your parents are invincible, so sitting in a hospital waiting room following an accident in which the wheel of a transport truck flew through the windshield of a modest four-door sedan didn't come with the same kind of dread I was feeling now. Then, I was young and stupid and didn't comprehend the gravity of the situation. Couldn't even begin to fathom what their loss would mean. That there would even *be* a loss. Now, it was different. My heart had remained closed off, protected, for so long. Natalie had worked her way in there, eventually, but Moustache had made it his home almost immediately.

"Ms. James? Did you hear me? He's awake."

I had a moment of stunned understanding, which was followed by a new batch of tears.

"I'd like to keep him for a few days. There are some tests I'd like to run."

"Can I see him?"

"He's in recovery. I'm afraid any excitement might be—"

"Please? He's all I have."

"I can let you see him from the window of the door. But I can't let you inside."

I nodded eagerly and followed the veterinarian to the doorway of the recovery room. Moustache was in a cage on the middle tier, flanked by a white fluff ball that I took to be either a poodle or a Bichon Frise and an orange cat. A small laugh escaped me.

"If you're worried about excitement, you might want to move that cat," I said to the vet.

"They can't see each other," he said with a smile. "Ms. James, I won't know for sure until I get some of the lab work back and run a few more tests, but I'm quite certain your dog may have been poisoned."

"What?"

"His symptoms are common to a number of disorders but are most likely associated with antifreeze toxicity." The confused look on my face propelled the vet to continue. "Antifreeze has a sweet taste that dogs and cats find very appealing."

"But he was in the backyard," I managed. "Even getting onto the driveway, I don't have any—"

"This kind of toxicity needs to be treated immediately if there's any chance of survival. Right now, Moustache is receiving fluids via intravenous to flush out any potential toxins from the kidneys. I've also inserted an intravenous catheter to administer an antidote that will halt any further poisoning. You probably can't see it from here, but there is a bit of blackness around Moustache's mouth. That's because I've given him a charcoal solution to absorb any antifreeze that might still be in the intestines. I'll know more tomorrow when I get the blood work back."

I couldn't speak.

"Ms. James, you mustn't be so hard on yourself. I can't tell you how many times I've thought my back gate was fully secured when it wasn't. It's a common mistake. Let's be grateful you found Moustache as quickly as you did and that you got him here in time."

"I don't use the gate. It hasn't been opened in weeks." I flashed back to the one time I could remember the gate being open—the police investigation. "The only way that gate could have been open is if someone opened it. And maybe whoever opened it gave him something."

"After I fully examine Moustache's stomach contents, we should be able to pinpoint how the antifreeze was ingested," the vet said in an attempt to placate me, rather than give any credence to my wild accusation. "I have every reason to believe Moustache is going to be fine. I'm sure we'll discover this was all a terrible accident and no one was out to hurt him."

"What about you?" Jeffers said.

"What about me?"

I was on the phone with Jeffers, having pulled myself together enough to hold a coherent conversation. The vet had finally succeeded in convincing me there was nothing else I could do for Moustache but go home and get some rest. Although I hesitated at first, the doctor's bribe of a hands-on visitation the next day did the trick and I was now settled on the living room couch, nursing the glass of wine I had started to pour when I was interrupted earlier by Shelagh Worthy.

"What if someone was trying to hurt you?" Jeffers said.

"Why would anybody want to do that?"

"You're a celebrity. People do crazy things sometimes."

"You think I have a stalker?"

"Would that be so far-fetched?"

"You're being ridiculous."

"Just be careful."

"Fine." I brushed off his suggestion but could feel it niggling away at the back of my mind.

"Now, what about Mrs. Worthy? How did she get your number, by the way?"

The "how" of the phone call had never occurred to me. "I have no idea."

"It's amazing how easy it is to track people down nowadays. Scary. What'd she say?"

Distracted by this new mystery, I repeated the phone conversation as best I could. As for the dark cloud that had passed so quickly over her during our phone exchange, Jeffers would have to take my word for it.

"And they never saw each other again?"

"I found that odd, too. But I guess if Duck blamed himself for not being there to stop the attack, and if he truly loved her in spite of the affair, he'd want to do whatever he could to facilitate her recovery, even if that meant letting her go without a fight."

"Or maybe the fight had already taken place."

"What do you mean?"

"You said Duck walked in on Olivia and Peter Wynn, presumably in bed together, and then left without a word?"

"Right."

"And the attack happened shortly after that."

"So?"

"So isn't it possible that Duck went back when Peter had left, confronted Olivia, and lost his temper? You saw the size of the man. If he was mad enough, think of the damage a person that size could do to someone like Olivia. It would be no wonder she didn't want to see him after that. And it would be no

Alexis Koetting

surprise he went along with that and gave her everything she asked for. She felt guilty about breaking his heart so she didn't press charges and he felt guilty about nearly killing her so he didn't contest her wishes."

I didn't want to believe Duck Worthy was capable of such violence, but Jeffers' explanation was neat and tidy and I had to admit I had no business judging what Duck was capable of after one meeting.

"So what do we do?" I asked.

"There's not much we can do. Charges were never laid."

"So he just gets away with it?"

"Everyone involved seems to be okay with that."

"I'm sure the woman in the ground might have a few choice words."

"We don't know for sure the bones are connected. I agree it seems an awful coincidence, but we can't go barging in on Duck Worthy and accuse him of murdering someone because he beat up his wife."

Jeffers was right. While our little goose chase had led us to uncover some details of Olivia's attack, it had done nothing to further our investigation of the bones. I couldn't help but roll my eyes as the word "investigation" ran through my mind. Jeffers and I, off on some Scooby adventure, trying to do what exactly? Unearth a past that obviously wanted to remain buried?

That night, I cried. I cried out of guilt and shame over all the broken promises Terri-Mae had endured and how I'd managed to disappoint her one last time before she died. I cried the tears my eight-year-old self had not been able to manage when my parents were killed. I cried for all the happy times I never allowed myself to have; the relationships I refused to let blossom; love I had rejected. And my dear Moustache, whom I had vowed to protect. I cried for it all.

CHAPTER 10

Moustache was released to me after spending three days being fussed over by all the veterinary technicians and hospital staff. His fan base rivaled mine, but while I was always uncomfortable with the attention, he reveled in it. Although I had been granted visitation during Moustache's stay, I was beside myself with impatience as I took care of the bill and waited for the jingle-jangle of his dog tags. I wanted him home.

"Ms. James," the vet called out in as hushed a tone as a calling-out could be, "I didn't want to tell you this over the phone and I wanted to wait until I had had a chance to discuss things with the police—"

"The police?"

He ushered me into a vacant examination room. "As we've discussed over the past few days, my original diagnosis of antifreeze poisoning was correct. What I haven't mentioned yet is when I fully examined Moustache's stomach contents, I found evidence of a dog biscuit, not yet digested. Some of the pieces tested positive for the toxin. You were right. Somebody laced the biscuit. I've reported the incident to the police. Unfortunately, there's not much else I can do. At this point we don't know if this was a random attack, or—"

"Someone was after Moustache," I finished.

Although I'd been in and out of conversation with the good doctor over the past few days, I'd never really noticed him. My sole focus was Moustache and the vet had been merely a mouthpiece, communicating what Moustache couldn't. But standing in the exam room, with the late afternoon sun peering through the blinds, he was more than Moustache's spokesman. He was a man in genuine pain over the revelation that Moustache's condition had been deliberately caused. And he was gorgeous! My feminine instinct suffered a moment's admonishment that I was "cruising" in the midst of this very serious situation. But only a moment's.

The sun highlighted the gold flecks in his chestnut hair. His green eyes were a perfect contrast. His build was slim, but athletic, no evidence of excess fat. I pegged him for a cyclist or an avid outdoorsman, due to the way the sun had obviously smiled on his face. I wondered if his nose had been a victim of one of his outdoor adventures as there was a crooked rugged-ness in his profile.

"Ms. James? Are you okay?"

I realized I was staring and, even worse, wearing a dumb grin. I made a quick mental note to have a word with my libido.

"I'm fine," I managed, looking anywhere but at him. "Just happy we figured this out. Hopefully in time to keep it from happening again to another dog."

Much to my relief, Moustache chose that moment to make his grand entrance, dragging a poor vet tech who struggled to control his leash.

"There he is!" the doctor cooed as he brought himself down to Moustache's level. Moustache, however, only had eyes for me. "You are free to go, boy," the vet continued. "Ms. James, if you have any further questions or . . . anything . . . please don't hesitate." And with a pat on Moustache's rump, the vet was gone.

"Or anything?"

I was in the greenroom with Adam.

"He meant about the poisoning," I deflected.

"Really! Bella James, ever since you started talking about this, you've had this stupid grin on your face."

"Because I am happy Moustache is okay!"

"Don't even go there, sister. That ain't no 'I love my dog' grin. That look has 'man' written all over it. And trust me, I know that look. I invented that look. So spill."

"I've never seen you with that look."

"What does that tell you about the men in this town? Now, quit stalling. Was there a wedding ring?"

A small laugh escaped me, betraying what Adam had already discovered.

"No," I surrendered, the blush rising in my cheeks.

"That doesn't mean anything," said a voice from the table next to ours.

Manda Rogers had one of the lead roles in the musical and a long resume to back up her chops. She'd also managed to put together a long resume of men with whom she had been involved.

"It may not mean anything to you, Manda," Adam said.

Manda was well aware of her reputation and took the comment in stride. Tales of her sexual exploits were well known in theatre circles and she had put her stamp on more than one failed marriage. She was unquestionably beautiful. A mane of red hair fell in a perfect cascade over her shoulders. A face and body that super models would pay for. She knew she was virtually irresistible and she wore her promiscuity with pride.

"Perhaps I should go see for myself," she said.

This was Manda's M.O. She didn't deem a man worth pursuing until someone else showed an interest. I could feel my temperature rise at the very thought of her waltzing her flawless self in front of Dr. Gorgeous.

"And why would you need to see a veterinarian?" asked

71

Adam, coming to my rescue. "Fleas bothering you again? Perhaps you finally want to get spayed?"

"I'm sure someone's got a cat I can borrow," she said, unfazed. She turned her brilliant smile on me. "If Rich Arborall is any indication of your 'type,' I'm sure the good doctor won't disappoint."

She sashayed out of the room. The gaze of a dozen sets of eyes watched her go.

"Cow." Me.

"Bitch." Adam.

"Sounds like the animal hospital is the perfect place for her after all." Leave it to Natalie to find the humor in every situation.

"Ah, it's fine," I insisted. "I don't have time to date anyway. The show is opening soon. I haven't even started rehearsals for *The Hothouse* yet."

"Whatever you need to tell yourself," said Natalie. "If you want to stand by and let little Miss Slut take your man because you're too scared to put yourself out there, then do it. But don't feed me lame excuses."

I did a mental comparison of how we would each be perceived by Dr. Gorgeous: Manda, perfect and sexy, versus me, eyes red from crying and nose snotty. "I don't want to talk about this anymore," I said.

For the next few minutes we discussed the basic things—Zack's current work, her guest position at the University of Toronto, my show, Terri-Mae's affairs. Eventually, the conversation came around to Duck Worthy and the role Jeffers believed him to have had in Olivia's assault. Our recent conversations had been all about Moustache's well-being and I realized I hadn't filled her in on Shelagh Worthy's phone call and my subsequent chats with Jeffers. She listened intently.

"So do we know if this has anything to do with the bones?" she asked when I'd finished.

"No, we don't," I said, exasperation coloring my response.

"What about this Peter guy?"

"What about him? He and Olivia were having an affair. She married him. That's it."

"Just hear me out. Go back to being Emma Samuel for a minute. When there's a victim of a crime, who's the first person the cops want to talk to?"

"Natalie," I said with a tone that screamed *Jeffers and I have been through everything!*

"Bella," she said, meeting me tone for tone.

"The husband. Or wife," I said, playing along.

"Okay. Who else?"

I let out a sigh. "The last person who may have seen the victim before the attack. Oh, I see. No one knows for sure if Duck went back to the house after finding Olivia with Peter."

"Which makes Peter—"

"Somebody worth talking to."

CHAPTER 11

As luck would have it, an opportunity to chat with the man of the hour presented itself sooner than I had expected. I'd gotten up early, accompanied Moustache on a long walk and, in an effort to distract myself from the fact it was the day of Terri-Mae's funeral, decided to treat myself and my Ken Follett novel to breakfast.

It wasn't fancy, but Silks was a favorite diner of the locals and offered a fabulous breakfast special for $3.69. Actors are always in search of a cheap meal and this one fit the budget perfectly.

I'd placed my order and was in the midst of retrieving Mr. Follett from my bag when the hostess showed Peter Wynn to a small table next to the big-screen TV. It was clearly not to his liking.

I was comfortably situated in a booth all by myself and hid behind Ken Follett, wondering whether engaging Peter Wynn in conversation would yield anything. Unfortunately, Jeffers had been hard to reach as of late and I hadn't had a chance to run my Peter suspicions by him.

"Bella James!"

I looked up to find Peter leaning over to kiss my right cheek.

"Peter. Nice to see you."

"When are you going to come to your senses and leave Dean and come over to my office, eh?" He slid into the booth opposite me.

Each time I met Peter Wynn, our rally went something like this: an attempt from him to poach me away from my agent, a polite brush-off from me, followed by an extension of an open invitation should I change my mind.

He flagged a waitress, then placed an order for coffee and the Big Breakfast. Of course. He was the type who always had to order the most expensive thing on the menu simply because he could afford it. Moments later my own breakfast arrived.

"Please start," he said, indicating my plate.

As if I'd actually entertained the thought of letting my bargain of a breakfast get cold while waiting for his veritable feast to arrive. Though charming, Peter Wynn was arrogant. I could see at once what would have drawn Olivia to him and what would have been the cause for their failed romance.

"No rehearsal today?" he asked

"We're in ten, out of twelves. We don't start until later," I said, referring to rehearsal days that essentially went from noon to midnight with a two hour break for dinner.

"Ah the dreaded cue-to-cue. I always hated those. So much waiting around for one technical drama or another to get figured out. Theatre is one of the oldest industries in the world. I can't believe, in all the years, they haven't been able to come up with something better."

"You were an actor?"

"For five minutes. Wasn't for me. Not enough money in it."

As the name suggests, actors are not required to run the play fully during a cue-to-cue rehearsal, but rather provide the lead-up lines and moments so the stage manager and the sound and light board operators can practice weaving their magic seamlessly into the piece.

I had finished one of my two poached eggs and was cutting into a well-done sausage when Peter's heaping plate was set before him. He made one last remark about the absolute dreariness of having to endure the multiple attempts at getting a cue just right, then moved on to prove himself the better man by telling me some story about how he had beaten the pants off my agent at a recent charity golf tournament. Second egg and sausage finished, I contemplated forgoing the home fries in favor of an early escape when Peter said, "I'm looking forward to seeing the show. Be there for Opening. Olivia's last, or so she says."

"What do you mean?"

"Oh, I don't believe this is really the end for her," he said. "She thinks she wants to retire, but I know Olivia. She'll be itching to do something again in a year or so. It's in her blood. Whatever she's feeling now, it will pass. The stage has not seen the last of Olivia Childries, I'm sure of that."

I couldn't help but pick up on a tinge of bitterness. For years Olivia had been one of Peter's most successful clients. I imagined it was his bank account more than anything that regretted her retirement.

Since we were on the subject of Olivia, I decided to try and get Peter Wynn to talk. With or without Jeffers' approval.

"It must be so hard for her," I said, gently inching forward. "I mean, the last time she did this show." Peter turned a steely gaze on me. I held firm. "I've heard about . . . what happened . . . and can only imagine—"

"What exactly can you imagine?" he asked disparagingly.

I was reminded of how Duck Worthy's demeanor had changed when Jeffers had broached the same topic. I also remembered how that exchange had ended up. I hurried on.

"I'm sorry. I'm not trying to be insensitive. I—"

"It happened a long time ago. And frankly, Ms. James, it's none of your damn business."

He fixed a cold, hard stare on me before crumpling his napkin and dropping it onto his unfinished plate. Without another word, he slid from the booth and strode out of the restaurant.

I crumpled my own napkin and chastised myself for not leaving well enough alone until I had a chance to talk to Jeffers. My little stunt had likely dashed any and all hopes of ever finding out if Peter figured into the circumstances surrounding Olivia's attack.

The waitress arrived to clear plates and deposit the bill on the table. I looked at the small piece of paper that held my total and couldn't help but chuckle to see my bill included Peter's breakfast. I guessed it served me right.

Terri-Mae's funeral had been a beautiful affair, according to Marie Coombs. Following a traditional church service, a reception had been held in Terri-Mae's home and she had been sent off in true east coast fashion. It was what she would have wanted and I was grateful Marie had seen to give her the celebration she deserved.

I was sure my absence was glaring but not too surprising. My youthful exploits had been well known in the neighborhood and more people than not pitied Terri-Mae her unfortunate role as my guardian. Many of Terri-Mae's friends still adopted stern demeanors at the mere mention of my name. I had not asked the Shaw Festival for time off to attend the funeral. I tried to convince myself it was because of logistics but knew, deep down, it was because I couldn't endure the looks of disappointment from Terri-Mae's nearest and dearest.

Marie told me she would take care of packing up Terri-Mae's house and would have her husband, Joe, a retired lawyer, look into the legalities of her affairs. Again, I expressed, as best I could, my gratitude. Not only for what Marie had done and was continuing to do, but also for the kindness she had shown my grandmother. She was a rare friend. I knew that because I had one of my own in Natalie.

Marie informed me that, per Terri-Mae's wishes, she had been cremated and buried alongside my parents and her late husband, my namesake. Marie asked if she should go ahead and have the headstone prepared with Terri-Mae's details. I had only visited the grave once, when my parents were buried, and never saw the stone with their names on it. My grandmother had visited regularly, however, and she'd want the memorial completed as soon as possible. I told Marie as much.

Thoughts of Terri-Mae danced around my brain, mingling with my earlier encounter with Peter Wynn, so I was surprised to emerge from my contemplation to find much of the cast of *Major Barbara* staring in my direction.

"We'd like to take it from Barbara's line, 'It's too melancholy.' " Caitlin's delicate voice emerged from the darkness of the theatre, helped along by a microphone.

Though I was clearly at fault, Caitlin's directive sounded as if she were beside herself with remorse at having to put me out.

"Of course," I said. "I'm so sorry." It was during one of the lengthy periods of waiting during a cue-to-cue that I had let my mind wander.

Olivia gave no notice of my lack of focus. She seemed to be in some daydream of her own. Adam, on the other hand, mouthed some silliness to me that happened to contain the words "doctor" and "gorgeous." To which I rolled my eyes and resisted mouthing my own sentiment back. I got into position and delivered the appropriate line. The scene progressed, the cue was called, and after a moment my blunder was forgotten and all was well again. In Shaw's world, anyway.

I still hadn't been able to reach Jeffers. I had left messages and emails, and the only response I got was a generic "Out of Office" reply. My thoughts immediately went to his wife and I hoped nothing had gone wrong with the pregnancy. Or perhaps

Raines had caught on to our shenanigans and fired him. I made a mental note to call him again on the break.

It felt like an eternity before we broke for dinner. Most of us were already bleary-eyed and I wondered how we would ever get through another four hours, let alone the following day's repeat of the schedule. Usually I devoured a good portion of a book during tech, but my mind was too busy thinking of other things and dreaming up extravagant scenarios.

"Are you heading to the greenroom?" asked the ever-persistent Jarod.

"In a minute." I nodded, wearily.

"Shall I save you a seat?"

I was tired and needed to save the rest of my energy for the remainder of the rehearsal. I did not have it in me to fight off Jarod Riley as well. "Sure," I said.

A brief cocking of an eyebrow was the only indication that my acceptance was a surprise. He followed that up with a slight bow of his head à la the character he played in *Barbara* and was off, no doubt, in search of the coziest corner the greenroom had.

"He's really very nice," said a voice at my left shoulder.

"I know," I said, turning to face Olivia. "If he was only interested in being nice, I wouldn't have a problem."

"It's amazing how men seem to need it spelled out for them, isn't it? When you're married, it's easy. You simply divorce them. Can't be clearer than that."

I realized she had given me a bit of an opening to continue my newest topic of interest, Peter Wynn. Every fiber in my being was screaming at me to leave it alone, but I convinced myself that I might be able to repair some of the damage I had done earlier. This moment was gift wrapped and waiting for me to tear it open.

"Are you and your ex-husband still friends?"

After the words were out of my mouth, it occurred to me that perhaps I should have specified which of her ex-husbands I was referring to. Olivia, however, didn't seem to need the clarification.

"He's still my agent," she said and then added with a smirk, "How friendly are *you* with your agent?"

She eyed me carefully. There was something in Olivia's gaze that suggested I was treading on precarious ground.

"Peter and I were never friends," she continued. "We were wonderful business partners. We still are. Unfortunately, that isn't enough to make a successful marriage. Once we both realized that, it was easy to move on. Our relationship is better now than it was when we were married."

"It couldn't have been *all* business," I said somewhat suggestively.

"Passion isn't everything, my dear," she said with a wink. "And to be honest, we were never very good at that either."

It was late when I fell into bed. In spite of the long day, I was nowhere near tired. My conversations with Peter and Olivia had set my brain abuzz. As far as getting anything that might help Jeffers and me along in our investigation, the exchanges had yielded little. But I couldn't shake the fact there was something to be gleaned. On one hand, I was puzzled over the comment Olivia had made about the sex not being very good. She'd had an affair with Peter during her marriage to Duck and had gone so far as to bring him into bed in her own home. Into the bed she shared with another man. She must have known there was a chance of getting caught. So, if it wasn't passion that led to her betraying her husband, then what? Did she really want out of her marriage to Duck Worthy so badly that she felt staging an affair was the only way? And once out of the marriage, why so quick to enter into a union with a man for whom her feelings were strictly professional?

This brought me to the other hand. Both Peter and Duck had reacted similarly when the night of the attack had been brought up. It was clear that neither man wished to talk about what may have occurred. And if they didn't want to talk about it, did that mean they were hiding something? Or was it too painful? Or was there something else? Something Jeffers and I were missing? The more I wrestled with these thoughts, the less things made sense. I felt like I was banging my head against a brick wall. And where the hell was Jeffers?

CHAPTER 12

When you only have one day off each week, getting all of the "have to" stuff out of the way as soon as possible is essential, especially if you're going to get to the "want to" stuff while it's still light out. I was standing in the Valu-Mart, handling a cantaloupe, when I noticed Dr. Gorgeous conducting his own thorough examination of an avocado. He caught me watching him.

Stupidly, I reached into thin air for something witty to say and, instead, came up with, "I never know how to tell if these are ripe or not."

He smiled a smile so dazzling, I had to hold on to the shelf to keep my knees from giving out. I returned a smile of my own, certain it would not have nearly the same effect. I was right, for in that moment he approached me with no apparent difficulty.

"Well, you happen to be in luck. Finding ripe cantaloupe is my specialty. The trick," he said, taking it from me and following his own directions, "is to look for a sweet, musky smell. Then you want to press it ever so slightly on the end, here. It should give a bit. You don't want it to give too much, otherwise it will be a bit on the mushy side." He discarded my melon and went through his routine with another. "It's early yet for cantaloupe, but if you have your heart set on one, I think you'll be happy with this one here."

"And I thought you just had a way with animals." I knew I was beaming and there was nothing I could do about it.

"Speaking of animals, how's my favorite patient?"

"He's great," I said. "Yeah, he's, um, great! He's—"

"Great?" he finished for me.

I laughed, self-consciously. He laughed perfectly.

I finally managed to regain some semblance of composure and we spoke briefly about Moustache. Dr. Gorgeous informed me there had been no other poisoning cases brought to his attention, which was both a relief and a cause for the hair on the back of my neck to bristle. We knew Moustache's attack had been on purpose, but the fact that no other dogs had suffered the same fate led me to wonder if Jeffers had been right, that Moustache's poisoning had been some kind of message.

"How's the show?" Dr. Gorgeous asked, snapping me out of my worrisome reverie.

"Going really well, thanks. We start previews this week. It'll be nice to get some audience response and a chance to iron out all of the kinks before we officially open."

Most theatres have two or three preview performances before a show opens. The Shaw Festival has close to two months of previews. It's a luxury.

"A client of mine offered me a ticket for Opening Night, so it had better be perfect by then," he teased. "There's a dinner before the show. Will you be going to that?"

He was referring to one of the dinners or lunches that were held before the opening of each show for the benefit of the theatre's Board of Governors, sponsors, high end donors, and the like.

"No. Only company members who have been with the Shaw for three years or more are invited to those."

"But you're one of the stars!"

I laughed. "Doesn't matter. It's tradition."

"I know there is usually a reception of sorts on the Opening Night so perhaps—"

My cell phone rang and I cursed silently.

"Excuse me," I apologized before answering. "Hello?"

"I need to see you."

"Jeffers!? Where have you been?"

"I'm on my way to your house."

"I'm at the grocery store."

"I'll be at your place in five minutes."

"Jeffers—" Too late. He had hung up. "I'm sorry," I said to Dr. Gorgeous. "I have to go."

"Is everything all right?"

"I don't know," I lied. From Jeffers' tone, things didn't sound good. "Thanks for your help," I said, indicating the melon.

"My pleasure." Another flawless smile. "It was nice running into you."

"Damn it, Jeffers," I said under my breath as I ran to the cashier, "this had better be good."

When I pulled into the driveway, Jeffers was leaning on the back of his car, holding a file folder.

"Jesus, Jeffers," I said, "you look terrible!"

He looked like he hadn't slept in days. The only color in his face was the purple in the circles under his eyes. His hair, usually stylishly mussed, was a mess, and his shoulders seemed to slump under an invisible burden.

"Where have you been? I've been calling and calling. I've been really worried," I said, a little irritated. "I didn't know if something had happened to the baby or if—"

"Bella," he said cutting me off. His use of my proper name rather than that of my TV personality stopped me in my tracks. "Can we go inside?"

Nodding and speechless, I led him into the house, where he promptly fell onto the sofa and held his head in his hands. I sat across from him in Moustache's chair. The file sat on the coffee table between us. From above, I heard Moustache jump off the bed. He appeared at the top of the stairs and did an expert downward dog before making his descent. I gave him a quick kiss and ruffled his snout, never taking my eyes off Jeffers. Moustache must have sensed the tension, for he quickly broke from my caress and looked toward Jeffers, who raised his head and let out a sigh before leaning back on the cushions.

"Come here, buddy," he said to the dog.

Moustache eagerly settled himself on the couch next to him, chin on his thigh. "Well, go on. Open it," he said.

I pulled the file toward me and took out the pages. I couldn't even begin to imagine what had put Jeffers into such a state and was a little reluctant to look. Jeffers was intently stroking Moustache's head.

Taking a deep breath, I read the top page. It was the record of the strange phone call Olivia had received weeks ago. I had completely forgotten Jeffers had promised to investigate the call. The report showed that Olivia's mysterious caller was not, as we had assumed, Erna Weins, but rather Shelagh Worthy. That wasn't odd in itself. Shelagh and Olivia had been friends since childhood. I racked my brains, trying to recall the part of the conversation I had overheard, which, I had to admit, wasn't really very much.

I waited for something to trigger my suspicion, but the more I thought about it, the more innocent the phone call seemed. I was unconvinced anything useful would come of the phone records, but Jeffers was clearly disturbed by something. Something I was clearly missing.

I flipped to the page detailing Shelagh Worthy's call history and hit the jackpot. Erna Weins had called *Shelagh* right after her talk with Jeffers. Shelagh, in turn, called Olivia. And, putting the rest of the pieces of the puzzle together, Olivia paid Erna a visit. A nice little circle. But what did it mean? I posed the question to Jeffers.

He reached over the coffee table to take the pages from me, dislodging Moustache's head from his lap in the process. The dog snorted his irritation before flopping over onto his back into his best Snoopy impression.

"Not this!" Jeffers was on the verge of fury. "Do you think I came all the way over here because of some phone records?"

"Jeffers, calm down."

"There," he said, sifting through the rest of the pages in the folder and pushing one toward me.

I read it three times before I met his gaze. Neither of us spoke.

"Oh, my God! Jeffers! Oh, my God!"

CHAPTER 13

"Where did you get this?" I said, my voice barely audible.

"Pathologist friend."

"I think you need to start at the beginning."

Jeffers ran his hands through his hair. "A few days ago I took a call. It was the coroner's office calling for Raines. He wasn't in so I took the information. They wanted to know if they could go ahead and dispose of the remains we found at your place."

"Dispose of them? Are you kidding me? This is huge! Why would they do that?"

Now it was Jeffers' turn to ask me to calm down. "Because when a body can't be identified, that's standard procedure."

"But according to this, she was identified," I insisted, pointing to the file.

"I know! Let me finish. I asked about the pathology report and was told all the paperwork had been submitted to Raines a few days earlier. Raines, of course, hadn't said anything about it to me, and I knew there was no chance in hell he was going to let me see the report, so I went to the inspector. Made up some excuse for needing to speak with him, then brought up the bones as casually as I could. He told me the lab had exhausted all efforts to I.D. her and he was closing the case. He was just waiting for Raines to bring him the paperwork with his signature. Can I have something to drink?"

For a moment, I didn't understand the question. My mind

was reeling from what I had read and from what Jeffers was saying.

"Bella?"

I grabbed a bottle from the wine rack as I moved toward the kitchen.

It was still early in the day, but I didn't think a glass of wine would hurt. Moustache followed me and sat hopefully at the back door. I let him into the yard, its gate now locked from the inside. Then I filled glasses and returned to Jeffers, who made no judgment at my choice of beverage.

"I don't understand," I said. "If the pathology report said no identification had been made, then how—"

"I'll save you the boring details. The long and the short of it is that I broke into Raines' office and took the report."

My mouth fell open. I was beginning to get a clear idea of what Jeffers had been doing these past few days.

"Relax," he said. "I made a quick copy and returned it. There's no way he could even know I'd been there." I made a face that suggested some kind of admonishment and he fired back with, "Bella, come on. We were really on to something and I needed to see the report for myself to be sure."

"And?"

"As you can imagine, there had been considerable damage to the bones, due to the amount of time they were in the ground. But the lab was able to determine cause of death as asphyxiation and able to corroborate what the coroner had already told us—the identity was that of a Caucasian female in her late twenties to early thirties, approximately five foot, eight inches. Dental comparisons proved to be inconclusive and, because no one knows who the victim is, and there's nothing to judge against, the lab was unable to run DNA tests."

"But if they were able to compare dental records, they must have had some leads. Why no DNA?"

Jeffers took a deep breath. "Remember at the start of all this, I told you I had a friend at the lab?"

"The pathologist friend?"

"That's the one. When I was looking at some of the autopsy photos, there was something off about the mouth. I called my friend and asked if I could stop by the lab to look at the details of the dental comparisons."

"You went to the lab? Oh, my God, Jeffers, if anyone tells Raines you were there! I mean looking at paperwork is one thing but actively engaging with the remains?"

"It was after hours. There was no one else there. And he's a good friend." We were both well aware of how many lines had been crossed. "I was able to get a good look at the tests and at the mouth itself. According to the records of the forensic dentist, our victim had an implant of some kind. A unilateral subperiosteal implant."

He said the name of the implant like it was supposed to mean something to me. I shook my head.

"The relative age of the bones and the age of the victim at the time of her death narrowed down the technology to the early nineteen-sixties. It normally would have been rare for someone so young to have undergone such a procedure but not impossible. The first-ever implant of that kind was done in the nineteen-fifties in the States. By the late fifties there were only a handful of dentists in Canada trained to perform such procedures. Dental records were requested from each of those dentists."

"All this was in the coroner's notes?"

Jeffers smiled wryly, shuffled through the papers on the table, and handed a page to me.

"One of those dentists was in Coldwater," he said. "I paid another visit to the town. The dentist is dead and his practice was taken over years ago. The receptionist told me the coroner's office had called, asking for dental records of all the patients who'd had the implant in our time frame, but dismissed them because all the patients were male. Except one. I brought the records to my friend and, boom, a positive I.D."

I had forgotten Olivia Childries' father had been a dentist. It made perfect sense he would have performed the smile-saving procedure on his daughter.

CHAPTER 14

"Jeffers, this is impossible."

"The dentals are a match!"

"But there's got to be some mistake. I mean, I saw Olivia yesterday! How can these be her bones?"

"I haven't thought that far yet," Jeffers admitted, "but there's no mistake. The teeth of our skeleton match records belonging to Olivia Childries. Of that I'm absolutely certain!"

"Okay, hold on. Let's just take a few steps back for a minute. Why would the forensic dentist have dismissed Olivia's records?"

"Think about it, Bella. Olivia Childries has been seen on stage for decades. Hell, she's right here in Niagara-on-the-Lake, starring in your show. What's the point in wasting time comparing her records to a Jane Doe when you know for a fact the records aren't going to match because their owner is very much alive? For once, I can actually see some sense in Skip Raines' thinking."

"Raines? What does Raines have to do with this? I thought this was the coroner's call?"

"Evidently, the coroner called Raines to get the official go-ahead on dismissing the records on the grounds that—"

"Right, because Olivia's alive."

"Only she's not."

"Jeffers, come on!!"

"What?"

"You actually think someone has been masquerading as Olivia

for thirty years? Without anyone noticing? There's got to be some other explanation."

"Do you have one?"

I didn't. "I need some air," I said.

We had been at it for hours. My body was stiff from hunching over file after file. My stomach grumbled, and my head was woozy from drinking wine on an empty stomach. I glanced at our empty glasses, then at Jeffers. No wonder he was entertaining such ridiculous thoughts.

Moustache was snoozing on the back deck.

I shook his leash and Moustache took to the lawn in a flurry of twirls. He raced past me into the house where he attempted a couple of pirouettes before allowing his rear end to hover slightly above the floor, too excited to do a proper sit.

"You coming?" I called over my shoulder to Jeffers.

He grumbled something I couldn't decipher. I decided to leave him be.

Opening the front door, I nearly jumped out of my skin. Olivia stood on the landing, her arm raised as if about to knock and, from the look on her face, I gathered her skin had loosened a little as well.

"Oh, God," I said, my hand to my heart. "I'm sorry. You surprised me."

"I'm so sorry. I didn't mean to startle you."

Olivia and I were speaking at the same time, overlapping in our joint shock. Moustache barked a few of his thoughts as well before sticking his head in Olivia's crotch.

I pulled Moustache into a more suitable position.

"I wanted to drop off a copy of the interview we did for the *Globe* a little while back," she said, petting Moustache's head. "They sent me an advance copy for my approval. They're going to run it just before the opening. I thought you might like to see it. They did a nice job. I think you'll be pleased."

I rambled on about something or other to do with the article but, at that moment, my thoughts went off on their own tangent. My mind's eye stared at Olivia, trying to find something in her that would make sense of what Jeffers had uncovered.

"Hi," Jeffers said, appearing in the doorway, exuding an energy that was in direct contrast to his disheveled appearance.

"Olivia, this is . . . my friend . . . um . . ."

"Andre," Jeffers said, extending his hand.

"Andre," I said, the name feeling foreign on my tongue, "this is Olivia Childries."

"Ms. Childries, it's a pleasure," he said. "I'm a big fan."

Olivia accepted Jeffers' compliment with complete charm and humility. Jeffers, in turn, was positively radiant. I shot him a quick "what's up?" look, which he answered with a Cheshire cat grin. Moustache slumped on the landing and snorted in protest to his walk's delay.

"I'm sorry, I don't want to keep you," Olivia said, handing me the envelope. "I see you were on your way out."

"We're in no rush," Jeffers said. "Do you have time for a drink? I'd love to hear about the show."

He stepped back and waved his arm in invitation. I felt my jaw drop. What was he doing?

"No, thank you. I really do have to run. But if it's not too much trouble,"—Olivia lowered her voice—"I would love to use your washroom." She smiled apologetically.

"Of course," I said, ushering her inside. The three of us stood in silence for what was really the briefest of moments, although it felt like an age.

"It's upstairs and to your left," Jeffers offered.

Olivia nodded her thanks, and went up.

"Didn't you say she lived here once?" Jeffers whispered.

"Yeah. Why?"

"She didn't know where the washroom was."

"What?"

"She had to wait to be told."

"She was probably being polite."

"I don't think so."

Jeffers and I were standing at the bottom of the stairs, looking like two children about to get caught with their hands in the cookie jar, when Olivia returned.

"Thank you," she said, oblivious to our tension. "I knew the large coffee was going to do me in, but I ordered it anyway." We all shared a laugh. "Well, I'll let you get on with your walk. Andre, it was a pleasure meeting you."

"The pleasure was all mine," Jeffers said through a roguish grin.

"What was that all about?" I said, turning on Jeffers as soon as Olivia pulled out of my driveway.

He dashed to his car and began rummaging around in his trunk.

" 'We're in no rush. Do you have time for a drink?' " I said, mimicking the fervent attention he'd showered on Olivia.

He pulled something I couldn't see from the trunk. "A glass would have been better," he said, "but I bet I can find something in the bathroom."

He raced by me and up the stairs to the bathroom. Moustache, who was still leashed and waiting on the landing for his promised walk, raised a curious eyebrow at me as Jeffers passed.

"I don't know," I said to the dog.

Unsatisfied, Moustache turned his attention back to the door. Within moments Jeffers reappeared, looking like the cat that swallowed the canary. In one hand he held a fingerprinting kit and, in the other, several lift cards on which I could see several dusty blotches.

"I'll need you to give me yours so I can rule them out, but I dusted everything that would have been touched recently so, hopefully—"

"That's why you invited her in for a drink? To get her prints?" I didn't know whether to be impressed or terrified. What were we doing? How far were we going to go?

"Bella, maybe, just maybe, the records are right and the woman who just left here isn't who she claims to be. Don't you want to know for sure?"

Jeffers took my silence for a yes.

CHAPTER 15

During the next few days my living room was transformed into our center of operations. Jeffers and I made note of all the things that struck us as interesting or unusual since the discovery of the bones. The section of wall above the fireplace in my living room had become the resting place of dozens of multi-colored sticky notes—the murder board. Of course, an actual murder had yet to be confirmed.

Jeffers worked covertly at the police station, which meant that things that would normally take a couple of hours were now looking at days before completion. The waiting was excruciating! Not to mention my daily interaction with Olivia. In everything she said and did I was looking for something that would result in a resounding, "Ah ha!" But so far, nothing suggested she was anyone other than who she said she was.

Having just returned from a preview matinee of *Major Barbara,* I took up my usual position opposite the fireplace and stared at the rainbow of musings and questions. My eyes settled upon one where Jeffers had scrawled something barely legible about Shelagh Worthy's phone call to me following our trip to Coldwater. He had questioned me at the time and I had dismissed it then and was about to do so again, but seeing the question written down made the answer seem more important. How *had* Shelagh Worthy gotten my phone number? When I moved from Montreal, I had joined the thousands of others who chose to forego a landline in favor of a cell phone.

A moment or two more of puzzling this out saw me bounding to the hallway to retrieve my script from my bag. I took a folded piece of paper from the sleeve of the binder that held the tattered pages of *Major Barbara,* and held it like the Holy Grail. On the first day of rehearsal, the stage manager distributed a contact list to all members of the company detailing every person's phone numbers and email address. I supposed any person on that list could have passed along my number, but I knew of only one who knew Shelagh Worthy: Olivia.

Thinking about one phone call brought another to mind: the phone call Olivia had received from Shelagh Worthy that afternoon at the theatre. I had dismissed its significance because of their long-standing friendship, but Jeffers' and my recent trip down memory lane reminded me that Olivia had been completely distracted after receiving it and had hightailed it to Erna's as soon as she had a chance. Erna may not have made the call, as we had initially suspected, but she was clearly a part of whatever it had been about.

Trying to fit Erna into the puzzle sent me to another crudely scribbled-on piece of paper and another question mark. The missing forty minutes. Jeffers' friend in the coroner's office had seemed quite certain that the bruising in the crime scene photos was consistent with a greater passage of time than the police report allowed for. Erna Weins had been the one to call the police that night. Either she had waited forty minutes to phone it in or she had lied about what she witnessed. She might look like a sweet little old granny, but I was starting to wonder if there was a wolf under that nightcap of hers.

Erna. Shelagh. Duck. Peter. The names repeated themselves in my mind. I closed my eyes and replayed every conversation I'd had with each of them. Both Duck and Peter had clammed up as soon as Olivia's attack was mentioned. I was certain they both knew a lot more about what happened that night. Erna's account of her involvement in Olivia's rescue was the same today as it had been thirty years ago. Not a word out of place. Shelagh Worthy was as busy making phone calls as she was making pies. And then there was Olivia. Or rather, if Jeffers' suspicions turned out to be correct, the woman passing herself off as Olivia. If the real Olivia Childries was murdered and buried in my backyard, then the current Olivia Childries was an even better actress than her reviews gave her credit for.

"Marjorie Adelman!" Jeffers announced as he walked into my living room, bearing a tray of lasagna.

Jeffers' wife, Aria, had taken to catering our sessions. She knew this case was the only chance Jeffers had of securing a place in Major Crimes and wanted to do whatever she could to further his cause.

"What?"

"Her name is Marjorie Adelman. I finally got a match off the fingerprints."

He wiggled a manila envelope into my hands before heading to the kitchen in search of plates and eating utensils.

Speechless, I hesitated. As much as I wanted to get to the bottom of this case, I was acutely aware of just how much our little investigation had cost me. I had admired Olivia's work for years. We had talked like friends on a number of occasions. Watching her command of the stage, and of the theatre as an art form and way of life, couldn't be anything but inspiring to any actor. She was a legend and whatever was in the envelope was bound to turn the theatre world on its ear.

"You okay?" Jeffers asked.

"Yeah," I said, opening the envelope's flap. "I'm just . . ." I shook my head and withdrew the papers.

A mug shot taken in 1980. The face that looked out at me from the photograph was different from the face I had come to know. The only things that were the same were the eyes.

"They did a pretty good job, didn't they?" Jeffers said.

"Who?"

"The facial reconstruction team." Jeffers drew two other photographs out of the envelope. "This one was taken of Olivia Childries shortly before, what we now know, was her death in 1982. And this one was taken about four years later at the Opening Night of *Mrs. Warren's Profession.*"

That had been Olivia's triumphant return to the stage following the attack. I looked at the pictures side by side and had to admit Jeffers was right. They had done an unbelievable job rebuilding the beaten face to Olivia's likeness. But they couldn't do anything about the eyes. And as similar as Marjorie Adelman now looked to Olivia, the eyes gave her away.

"So what's her story?" I asked, still looking at the three photographs.

"She was in the system for a domestic disturbance. She and her husband went at it one night. Neighbor called it in," Jeffers said, reading from the police report. "Evidently, Marjorie's husband made regular use of his wife as a punching bag."

"Do we know anything else?"

"I ran her name and saw that we do have a small file on her. A quick trip to the archives and voilà," he said, brandishing a second manila envelope from his backpack.

This envelope contained a couple of pages detailing calls made to police from Adelman, reporting her husband's abuse. The list was lengthy. There was a copy of a restraining order she had taken out against him in June of 1981. There was also a copy of a police report filed in July of that same year that told of police responding to a call from the Greater Niagara General Hospital about Marjorie Adelman having been severely beaten. A note was made on the report that Marjorie had been discharged from the hospital after a few days and taken to Mercy Lodge women's shelter. There was nothing else.

"So we don't know anything about what happened to Marjorie from July of 1981 to when she, presumably, killed Olivia and took her place in August of 1982?"

"We know she wasn't working alone."

"And how do we know that?"

"The beating. There's no way it was self-inflicted. Someone else had to have been there that night."

"Of course! The reconstructive surgery! She needed Olivia's face if she was going to take over her life." I shook my head. "You think it might have been her husband? You think they're in this together?"

"It's possible," Jeffers said, rifling through some papers until he found what he was looking for. "Lance Adelman did nine months for violating the restraining order. He was out early April, eighty-two."

"But why Olivia? Why go to such extremes?"

Jeffers shrugged. "Money?"

"No," I said. "Olivia's career had barely begun to take off. She didn't have anything. Not then."

"I don't know, Samuel," Jeffers said, shaking his head. "And we're not going to find all the answers tonight. But at least now we know what we're looking for."

CHAPTER 16

"That's not for you, I hope."

I turned around in my seat to find Manda Rogers raising an eyebrow at me from the next table and pointing to my laptop.

"No," I said, closing the computer, irritated that I hadn't taken more care to see who was around me before I had booted up.

I had been researching battered women and, more specifically, Mercy Lodge. Manda sniffed at my response, clearly expecting more of an explanation.

"I'm doing some research," I offered after a moment's hesitation.

"For a role?"

"Something like that," I said, noncommittal.

"A movie? A return to TV? Theatre not really turning out to be your thing?"

I smiled. I couldn't help but be amused by her little games. "Actually, Manda, I don't suppose you've read *The Hothouse*," I said, referencing the play I would begin rehearsing in a month's time.

The play had nothing to do with battered women, but I took the chance Manda didn't know that. If she did, I supposed I could somehow tie it to the offstage rape.

She took a moment to primp her hair. "Isn't that the one with you and all the men?"

I nodded. My character, Miss Cutts, was the only female in

the cast of seven.

"Well, I'll leave you to it," she said, gathering up the remains of her lunch and throwing the strap of her bag over her shoulder. "By the way, I'm really looking forward to seeing you in *Major Barbara*. I'm coming to the dinner before the show. I have the most scrumptious date. As a matter of fact, I think you know him. The vet?"

I flashed back to my conversation with Dr. Gorgeous over a cantaloupe. He had mentioned that a client of his had invited him to the opening. I had assumed it was some rich patron of the theatre. I thought he, of all people, would be able to see Manda's seductions for what they really were. I could feel myself start to droop. Manda was still talking.

". . . anyway, if I don't see you beforehand, break-a-leg."

"What was that all about?" Adam had caught Manda's grand exit and made a beeline for me.

"I can't stand that woman," I said, before launching into the tale of Manda's latest conquest.

Manda and I shared a dressing room. Thankfully, we were never in it at the same time. As *Barbara* was this evening's on-stage offering, all of my costumes had been brought in and my personal effects occupied the dressing room table. Manda's outfits were stored in the wardrobe room and her personal items were stowed away in a little box bearing her name. The lid of her box was askew, as if tempting me to take a chunk out of her lipstick or spit in her mouthwash.

A visit from Olivia brought a halt to my petty scheming.

"Oh good, you're here."

"Hi," I said, trying to appear as normal as possible while my insides turned to jelly.

I had successfully managed to avoid social interactions with

Olivia in the days since Jeffers and I had uncovered her true identity.

"I feel like we've been just missing each other lately. I've barely seen you."

"I know." I tried desperately to echo her frustration and disappointment. "Come sit," I said, pulling out another chair. My internals started convulsing.

"We'll have to fix that," she said, taking the seat. "I'm holding my annual Easter Dinner on Monday and I'd love for you to be there."

"Oh! Oh, Olivia, I don't really celebrate—"

"That's all right. I know we all have our own ideas about religion and faith. This isn't about that. Easter is a celebration of new life. Of new beginnings. Those are themes that are very important to me. When one has had a near-death experience," she said, lowering her voice and glancing quickly at the door, "getting a second chance is a gift unlike anything else in the world. Not a day goes by that I'm not grateful. And so I celebrate it!" She smiled broadly.

Thinking about what her new life had cost the real Olivia Childries, I found it hard to share in her joy.

"Bella, is everything all right?"

"I'm sorry," I said, pulling myself together. "You've never mentioned the attack before. It caught me a little off guard."

"No, I don't like to talk about it." After a deep inhale she smiled warmly again. "But it's hard to keep some things private when they've been on the front page of every newspaper in the country."

"I guess that's true," I said, this time meeting her smile with one of my own.

"So," Olivia said, taking my hand in hers, "I've been celebrating my new beginning every Easter and this year I want you to be there. I won't take no for an answer."

"In that case, what can I bring?"

"Oh, good!" She clasped her hands together as she rose and made for the door. "No need to bring anything. Unless of course you want to bring a date? What about that lovely man I met at your place? Andrew?"

"Andre?"

"Oh, yes, Andre. The more the merrier," she said and gave a little wave.

I barely had time to contemplate what I had just gotten Jeffers and myself into when there was another knock on my door. Taking my head out of my hands, I looked up to see Jarod Riley lounging in the doorway.

"Hey," I said as casually as I could. "What's up?"

He fiddled with an envelope. "I was at a fundraiser the other night and they gave out a bunch of door prizes and I was the lucky winner of a gift certificate to the Grille on King."

My stomach turned while I waited for the inevitable invitation. I knew my greenroom charity would come back to haunt me.

"I was wondering if you'd like to help me put it to good use. I was thinking maybe tonight? After the show?"

"Oh, Jarod, that's so nice of you but . . ."

In the pause that followed I thought about how my day had panned out so far. Manda Rogers was dating Dr. Gorgeous and Jeffers and I had just been invited to the annual celebration Olivia's imposter held in honor of their switcheroo. The day was really calling for a cherry.

"Jarod, I'd love to."

"Was it as bad as you were expecting?"

Natalie was trying to be empathetic but the excitement coursing through her veins at the thought of me having gone on a date was impossible to disguise.

"Actually, no." A little squeal from the other end of the phone. "Stop," I said, throwing a wrench into her celebration. "It wasn't *as* bad. It was still bad."

"Oh, Bel, come on!"

"Natalie, he's one of those actors who have nothing else in their lives. Everything he talked about had to do with who he's worked with and what he's worked on. Name drop, name drop, name drop. I would have had just as much fun if I'd had dinner with his resume."

"Maybe he was trying to play things safe on the first date. Keep the conversation to what you both have in common."

"Natalie, you're really grasping at straws!"

"I'm just saying, Bella, sometimes I think you don't really give people a chance. You judge early on, you convince yourself you have everyone all figured out, and you leave very little wiggle room for anyone to exist outside of the little box you've put them in."

"I don't—"

"Yes, you do. Speaking as someone who got out of the box, Bel, if there is someone who is willing to take a chance on you, it only seems fair that you do the same. And if it doesn't work, it doesn't work. Was the food good at least?"

I had just hung up from Natalie when the phone rang in my hand. Jeffers. Moustache looked up at me from his cushion on the floor, walked two circles on top of his bed and plopped himself down with his back to me.

"Hi," I said. "What's up?"

"I got an address for Marjorie Adelman's husband. Thought we could drop in tomorrow and have a chat. You up for it?"

"Sure. After four, okay?"

I didn't have a show the next day, but because we were still in previews, the director was able to call rehearsals.

"Perfect. I also made an appointment with the Executive Director of Mercy Lodge. I'll see if I can switch it to later. We can make an evening of it."

"Great," I said, unconvincingly.

"You don't have to do this, you know."

"I know. I want to. I do."

While a part of me wanted to bury this case in the hole in my backyard and run from it as fast as I could, I felt a duty to Olivia, the real Olivia, to find her true story and put her to rest.

"You're not the only one with news," I said, and filled Jeffers in on Olivia's annual Easter celebration.

"Fantastic," he said. "I'll make a list of things for you to be on the lookout for while you're there. With any luck—"

"Put your pen down, Sherlock," I said. "She invited you, too."

CHAPTER 17

Lance Adelman ran an electrical supplies store in Thorold, a city about forty minutes southwest of Niagara-on-the-Lake. Jeffers and I arrived shortly before five. A bell attached to the door announced our entrance into the shop.

"Just about to close up. Make your business quick," was the gruff response that answered the bell.

"Charming," I whispered to Jeffers.

I was trying to come into the interview with an open mind, but everything I knew about Lance Adelman, from his abusive tendencies to his questionable customer service, made it hard not to prejudge.

He was behind the counter, looking over the day's receipts and took little notice of us as we made our approach. He was a large man, mid- to late sixties. I couldn't help but compare him to Duck Worthy. The two men were of a similar height and build but, where Duck was solid muscle, Lance Adelman had evidently paid little attention to his physique. His hair, the antithesis of Duck's fullness, formed a small, grey fringe at the base of his skull. Given how little hair remained on his head, I was surprised to see a few flakes of dandruff adorn his shirt collar.

"Can I help you find something?" he asked, gaze still on the receipts.

"I hope so," Jeffers answered and took out his badge. "I'm with the Niagara Regional Police. This is my partner."

Immediately I tried to adopt my best Emma Samuel attitude. Adelman looked up quickly. A hand smoothed over the top of his bald head.

"What's this about?" Adelman asked.

"You're Lance Adelman?" Jeffers readied his notebook.

"What's this about?" Adelman's gaze shifted from Jeffers to me and back to Jeffers.

"We have some questions about your wife, Marjorie."

"She dead?"

Jeffers and I exchanged a look.

"Mr. Adelman, when was the last time you saw your wife?" Jeffers said.

"Look, I ain't done nothin'. I ain't seen her in years."

"Can you be more precise?"

"Since before I went to prison," Adelman said after a pause. "Since you're a cop, I reckon you know when that was."

Jeffers allowed himself a knowing smirk. Adelman's eyes narrowed in response.

"Mr. Adelman, after you got out of prison, did you and your wife have any contact?"

"I just told you, I ain't seen her."

It was clear Adelman was quickly losing patience with Jeffers but had enough experience with the police to know better than to lose his cool.

"There are other ways of making contact, Mr. Adelman."

"You didn't answer my question. Is she dead?"

"And you didn't answer mine."

Adelman gave an amused grunt. "No, I ain't seen or heard from Joy since I got out."

Jeffers and I waited for him to go on.

"I got knocked around pretty good when I was inside. Makes a man look at himself. I knew why I was there. I knew what I done. I deserved every punch and kick I took." Adelman looked down. "I tried callin' when I got out but the number was out of service. Went by the house and all her stuff was gone. I finally got it out of her sister that she was in some women's shelter. I went by, but the woman at the shelter wouldn't tell me anything about her. Wouldn't even tell her I was there. That's it."

He adopted a wide-legged, crossed-arms, done-talking stance. I wasn't sure I entirely bought in to his whole "changed-man" story, but I gave him the benefit of the doubt.

"Mr. Adelman, you mentioned that Marjorie has a sister," I said.

"Yeah. Violet."

"Were she and Violet close?" I stole a quick look at Jeffers and caught an almost imperceptible nod. I could tell we were sharing the same train of thought. Perhaps Marjorie still kept in touch with her sister.

Adelman shrugged. "They were sisters. You know, close one day, hating each other the next."

"Do you know where we might find Violet?"

"Died a coupla years ago. Fire. I read about it in the paper."

My heart sank as our one and only lead went up in flames.

Jeffers said, "Mr. Adelman, where were you on the night of August third, 1982?"

"What? How the hell am I supposed to know? That was over thirty years ago! Do you remember where *you* were?"

"Thank you for your time." Jeffers closed his notebook and turned to go. I followed suit.

"Wait a minute. Wait a minute," Adelman said as he came out from behind the counter. "Is Joy . . ." He seemed overcome by emotion. "Marjorie? Is she dead?"

Marjorie Adelman was technically alive but had been living someone else's life for almost half of her own. She was, in no way, the woman Lance Adelman had married.

Jeffers turned to the anxious Adelman. "I'm sorry."

"He's not involved," Jeffers said to me.

"I agree. His reaction to the question of his whereabouts on August third was genuine."

When keeping secrets, there is always the paranoia that someone will find you out. People tend to cover their track as best they can. Create alibis or excuses. Fill in details. Just in case someone at some point should ask a question about what they're hiding. They'd always be ready, even decades after the fact. Lance Adelman's sincere bafflement at being asked to recall a random day in his past proved his innocence more than any answer he could have given.

Jeffers and I were en route to Mercy Lodge.

"So we're back to square one in terms of accomplices," I said.

"It could be anybody," Jeffers said. "We don't know enough about Marjorie Adelman yet to connect her to anyone specific. All we know is whoever helped had to have been capable of administering that beating."

My mind flashed to Duck Worthy. He certainly had the size and the strength needed to overpower a woman of Marjorie's stature. And the initial report had mentioned that he'd had a towel wrapped around his hand. Maybe I'd been too quick to dismiss him as a possible suspect. I had been distracted by what I had taken for years of grief, but maybe he'd simply been covering his tracks.

"Duck Worthy," I said to Jeffers.

"That would certainly explain why 'Olivia' called a stop to the investigation into the attack and why no charges were ever laid."

"And why Duck let his marriage go so easily."

"And why he refused to talk to us about that night. But I

thought you were on Duck Worthy's side in all of this?"

"I have to admit it makes sense. Olivia wasn't a random victim. She was chosen for a reason, and killed with the intent of Marjorie taking over her life. We don't know yet whether Marjorie knew Olivia, but if she didn't it could only mean that the person who helped her did. And this person had to have been someone who could wield a beating so severe it would necessitate having her face rebuilt."

"Duck Worthy certainly fits the physical bill."

"Shelagh Worthy said Duck and Olivia had loved each other since they were children."

"Some people grow together, others apart."

"Far enough apart that one member of the party is driven to murder?"

"Olivia was having an affair, let's not forget that. She had clearly moved on from Duck. Perhaps Duck chose to move on in a different way."

"Why not just divorce her?"

"Maybe Marjorie made Duck an offer he couldn't refuse," Jeffers said with a twinkle in his eye. "Marjorie has been keeping up this charade for thirty-some-odd years. In the spotlight no less. She clearly has something invested. And whatever it is might have been the out Duck Worthy was looking for."

Although they had shelters located all over the Niagara region, the administrative offices of Mercy Lodge were located in Niagara Falls. I glanced at the clock on Jeffers' radio, 5:48 p.m. Judging from the handful of cars that remained in the parking lot, I guessed that most of the administrative staff had called it a day. Jeffers parked in a spot nearest the entrance and took a manila envelope from the back seat.

"You sure do know how to show a girl a good time," I said before getting out of the car.

The entrance to the building was protected by an electronic lock that could only be opened by someone inside. Jeffers rang the bell and announced himself and a clicking noise gave us permission to enter. Pictures of smiling women and children adorned the walls of the hallway, along with some certificates of recognition and awards of excellence from the Niagara Region and the provincial government. I thought about how much Mercy Lodge had evolved since Marjorie Adelman had used its services. What did that say about society that a company like this one should expand out of necessity?

"Detective Jeffers?" A woman appeared in the reception area. "I'm Nancy Allenby," she said, offering her hand.

"Ms. Allenby, thank you so much for taking the time to meet with us," Jeffers said shaking the extended hand. "This is my partner, Ms. James."

The handshake came to me.

"I don't know if I'll be of any help," Nancy Allenby said as she led us through a maze of cubicles where a few people were working late.

I placed her in her mid- to late forties. She wore very little makeup and her hair was extremely short. She was taller than Jeffers and me, even without her high heels, and I had the feeling she would have been more comfortable in running shoes. Everything about her screamed "athlete."

"Please, have a seat," she said when we'd reached her office.

She made no effort to close the door. Jeffers and I settled onto a brown leather sofa while she moved to retrieve some papers from her desk before sinking into one of the two matching bucket chairs opposite us.

"You realize, Detective, that all of the women who come to us are guaranteed complete confidentiality?"

"I do, and, as I said on the phone, this information may be pertinent to an investigation we are conducting."

Nancy Allenby smiled. "Many of our women are involved in investigations of some kind."

"Ms. Allenby, in 1982 a woman was murdered," Jeffers said, ignoring the undercut. "The case was never solved. Recently we've come into some new information regarding this case and have reason to believe that the woman I spoke to you about, Marjorie Adelman, might have a connection to the victim."

Jeffers had been masterful in the way he appealed to Nancy's sympathies for women who had experienced violence. In no way did he allude to the fact that Marjorie Adelman was the aggressor in this particular case.

"Ms. Allenby," Jeffers continued, "Marjorie Adelman may have the information we need to close this case and put whoever's responsible behind bars. Unfortunately, our last known location for Ms. Adelman is Mercy Lodge during the summer of the same year."

This was a lie, of course. We knew exactly where Marjorie Adelman was. What we didn't know, and what we needed to inch out of Nancy Allenby, was who Marjorie Adelman used to be. Who she was when she decided she needed to become Olivia. We needed to fill in the gap between the time Marjorie came to the shelter and the time of the murder. We were sure Nancy Allenby had that information. Some of it at least. And we were sure that if we could just get her in the sharing mood, we'd finally have some of it, too.

She took a long look at the papers in her hand, crossed and re-crossed her legs, and finally looked to Jeffers and me.

"Detective, Ms. James," she started, "I don't know how much you know about the women who come to us or how much they've endured before they seek our help. It requires tremendous courage and comes with considerable risk. We are committed to seeing each and every one of them through every phase of their recovery. And that does not end when a woman is ready to leave one of our shelters. Whether it was yesterday or thirty years ago, we are committed to ensuring the safety of these women."

"Ms. Allenby, we—"

"I'm sorry for the woman who was killed. I truly am. But I'm afraid I can't help you. Any breach of confidentiality could put Ms. Adelman at risk. I'm sorry."

She stood, signaling an end to our interview.

"Thank you very much for your time," Jeffers said.

Again, we went through the motion of shaking hands although the action felt much more labored than it did when we had arrived.

We made our way back through the network of cubicles, unescorted this time, and had reached the exit when a woman called out from the reception area and hurried toward us.

"I'm sorry," she said in a hushed voice, "I wasn't eavesdropping, but I couldn't help but overhear some of your conversation with Ms. Allenby." She took a quick peek over her shoulder. "If you give me a few minutes and meet me at the Starbuck's on the corner, I think I might be able to help."

CHAPTER 18

Jeffers and I waited close to fifteen minutes and were starting to think that our helpful miss had had a change of heart when she bustled through the door, cheeks flushed, eyes wide with nerves.

"I'm sorry. It took me a little longer than I thought to close down my station," she said, joining us.

"It's fine," Jeffers reassured her. "We're in no rush."

She gave an anxious nod.

"Ms. . . . ?"

"I'd rather not say. Is that okay?"

"Of course," I said as warmly as possible. I was worried that any push might send the poor thing running before she could tell us what she knew.

"Can I get you something?" Jeffers offered.

"No. Thank you. I don't plan on being here long." After a quick intake of breath she said, "You were asking about Marjorie Adelman."

"Yes, we have reason to believe—"

"I heard. I don't mean to be rude but talking to you could get me into a lot of trouble. I'm breaking confidentiality."

Jeffers and I exchanged looks and silently agreed to let this woman talk until she didn't anymore.

"The shelter saved my life. I believe in everything they do. So much that I started to work for them. At first it was a part of my recovery. A way to give back, you know? But then it became so much more to me. I really love what I do and I don't want to jeopardize that."

Jeffers and I offered as much understanding as we silently could.

"My brother was murdered," she continued. "They never found the person who did it so I also understand what it's like to live without closure. That's why I'm here. If it helps bring your murdered woman's family some . . . rest . . ."

"Thank you," I whispered and covered her hands with one of mine.

"When I came to the shelter, Marjorie had already been there for some time. Our rooms were next to each other and, eventually, we developed a friendship. But there was a woman. A volunteer. Sherry, um, Cheryl . . . Bowman, I think her name was. She and Marjorie were really close. Marjorie and I would only talk when she wasn't there. She had this kind of control over Marjorie. That's not the right word. It just seemed that she didn't want Marjorie getting too close with any of the other girls. So other than the two of us, Marjorie kept pretty much to herself."

Gently, I asked, "Did she ever confide in you?"

"She was terrified. Apparently her husband had found out where she was and was making threats. He'd come by several times a week. Ms. Bowman always dealt with him. He even roughed her up a bit once."

Jeffers and I looked at one another. Lance Adelman had told us that he went to the shelter once to make amends. He was turned away and never went back.

"Then one day, Marjorie was gone," Miss No Name whispered.

"What do you mean?" Jeffers asked.

"She vanished. Didn't say a word to anyone. I think they moved her to a different shelter. Because of her husband maybe. I remember asking Ms. Bowman if she knew anything but—"

"Do you remember when Marjorie left the shelter?" I asked.

"It was the beginning of August, 1982. I remember because I had a calendar in my room with pictures of Italy. I've always wanted to go," she said with a small, self-conscious laugh. "I had just changed the month and there was a picture of Venice. I remember Marjorie admiring it. I didn't see her again after that."

The timeline fit.

"Was any of this useful?" she asked.

"Absolutely," I said, on top of Jeffers' "Ma'am, you have no idea."

This poor woman had taken a big chance in talking to us and we began falling all over ourselves in our efforts to make sure she knew how much we appreciated her coming forward.

"One last thing, if you don't mind," Jeffers said. "Did Marjorie ever mention the name Olivia Childries?"

Miss No Name took a long time before answering. "No. I don't remember ever hearing that name. Why? Is that the woman who died?"

Jeffers offered a reassuring smile and rose from his seat. "Ma'am, thank you so much. You've been very helpful."

One could practically see the relief spilling over her as the interview came to its end. Jeffers and I were treated to a quick good-bye before watching her hurry out of the restaurant.

"That son of a bitch lied to us," Jeffers said referring, I knew, to Lance Adelman.

"It doesn't matter," I said. "Even if he did continue to terrorize his wife after he got out of prison, it doesn't change the fact he had no idea about Olivia's murder. In fact, it gives us our motive."

"How do you figure?"

"What better way to escape your abusive ex than to disappear. And what better way to disappear than . . ." I let Jeffers finish the thought.

He smirked. "Looks like you did learn a few things on that TV show of yours."

I threw a napkin at him.

"Okay, so we know Marjorie Adelman left the shelter at the beginning of August," he said.

"Which means she was free to kill Olivia on the night of the third," I finished.

"Right," he said, "and we have a possible motive. But we still don't know how she's connected to Olivia or who her accomplice was."

"Or how she got out of the shelter with no one seeing her. And where did she go when she left the shelter?"

" 'Detective Samuel' is on a roll tonight, ladies and gentlemen."

I rolled my eyes at his teasing but, inwardly, gave myself a pat on the back.

"I think we'll be able to answer that when we find the man who helped her," Jeffers said.

"Don't you think we should take this to Raines?" I asked, gingerly.

Jeffers scoffed.

"I know the man's a jerk but this is really big!"

Jeffers looked away.

"Come on," I persisted. "This is murder. And fraud. And God knows what else. This is bigger than the two of us. I know you want to do this on your own. To prove your worth to Major Crimes. But—"

"Not Raines! This is a thirty-year-old case that I have . . . that *we* have cracked wide open. And we're close, Bella. We are close to figuring this out. Don't you feel it?"

People in the restaurant started to look.

"I don't want Raines anywhere near this so he can swoop in

and take the glory that is rightfully mine," Jeffers continued.

"Wow," I said, quietly. "So this is about glory?" I was stunned by the ferocity in his voice and the hostility that had taken over his demeanor.

"I didn't mean it like that," he said, finding some calm and lowering his voice. He held his head in his hands. "I didn't mean it like that," he said again.

"I know."

Jeffers was a good man and an exceptional Detective Sergeant. It's human nature to want our accomplishments recognized. It's not always one of our most attractive attributes, to be sure, but it's inherent in all of us. How many times had I acted circles around another actor only to have them walk away with the glowing review?

"What about someone else?" I asked when the dust had settled. "The Inspector? If we take it to him, he'll see this is all you. Even if Raines ends up involved, the Inspector will know it was you who made this case."

"Going over Raines' head. That's bound to make me even more popular."

"Who cares? He's retiring in a couple of months, right? Besides, if you prove yourself to the Inspector there's nothing Raines could say to hurt your chances of staying in the division."

Jeffers offered up a reluctant smile. "Okay," he said. "But *after* the Easter thing at Olivia's. We might be able to learn something there, and the more we have to show the Inspector, the better."

CHAPTER 19

Every Easter Terri-Mae made this ridiculous cake in the shape of a lamb. She would present it on a field of shredded green coconut dotted with jellybean flowers. It had been a favorite of my father's when he was a child and she thought she'd continue the tradition with me. Underneath its white, frosted fleece was a simple pound cake, and I always felt a little uncomfortable cutting into its body, but Easter was never Easter without it.

When I moved out, she sent the mold with me. I'd never made the cake, but in anticipation of Olivia's Easter feast, I found myself digging it out of a box and soon I was up to my elbows in cake batter and green food-coloring. The sound of a car door slamming told me Jeffers had arrived to pick me up for the big event.

Jeffers let himself in and was greeted by the sight of Moustache's rear end high in the air as he squeezed his head and shoulders under a shelving unit, trying to reach a jellybean that had fallen.

"I've been called worse," Jeffers said to Moustache's elevated back end.

Moustache ignored him, refusing to be distracted from his mission. A quick trot into the living room moments later suggested the dog had been victorious and wouldn't let his prize be taken away from him. I watched his shaggy rump wiggle triumphantly out of sight and turned back to Jeffers to find that he had taken advantage of Moustache's escape to help himself to one of the jellybeans on the lamb's coconut bed.

"Stop!" I said, slapping his hand as he reached for another. "Besides, I thought you were cutting out sugar?"

"Not on special occasions," he said. "So what's with the, um"—he took a moment to get his smile under control— "sheep?"

"It's a lamb," I said.

"Ah," Jeffers said, fighting off the grin that was trying to force its way onto his face.

"We all have traditions, Jeffers, and this is one of mine," I said, "and I would appreciate if it could remain untouched until it gets where it needs to go."

Jeffers' grin was now full-on and infectious, and I could feel the ends of my own mouth beginning their own upturned motion. A moment later we were both laughing outright.

"I'm not sure Olivia is going to like being upstaged by a lamb," Jeffers said as his laugh dwindled to a chuckle.

"She deserves it," I said. "This whole evening is sickening. She calls it 'celebrating new life' but it's really celebrating getting away with murder. So what's the plan? What are we looking for?"

"Anything that can tie her to Marjorie. People always keep mementos. There has to be something about her past she would have wanted to hold on to. A letter; a photograph. She may have kept up some correspondence with her sister before she died."

"Okay. Anything else?"

"Just keep your eyes and ears open, Samuel. It's a celebration! People overindulge, they relax, they start letting their guards down, and when that happens, people start talking."

"You think an extra glass of wine or so is going to be our ticket to the truth?"

"I hope so," Jeffers said, brandishing two bottles of Amarone from the bag he carried. "That's why I brought the good stuff."

"Why, Bella James, you've come to me at last!" Peter Wynn remarked as he answered the door at Olivia's house.

"Hello, Peter," I said politely, going through the charade of the double kiss.

"What in God's name is that?" he asked, eyeing the lamb cake. Before I had a chance to answer, Peter cut me off. "Peter Wynn," he said, extending his hand to Jeffers.

Jeffers offered his name but Peter trampled over it.

"I keep hoping Bella here will come to her senses and come over to my agency. I could give her twice the career Dean can. By the way," he said, resting his arm across my shoulders and leading me down Olivia's hallway, disregarding Jeffers completely, "I never did thank you for that lovely breakfast."

He punctuated his gratitude with a meaningful squeeze of my shoulder. There was no mistaking its implication. I was not to mention our meeting to our hostess, nor was I to broach the subject again.

"Our Bella sure likes to play the field," announced Peter as we emerged into Olivia's living room. "Or maybe I should say *in* the field. 'Bella had a little lamb, its fleece was white as—' "

"Peter, you're such a boor." Olivia giggled as she approached us, arms outstretched.

Peter left us and moved to make himself a drink.

"Welcome! Welcome!" sang Olivia. "I'm so glad you could make it."

"Wouldn't miss it," Jeffers said, his double meaning not lost on me.

I grinned in spite of myself.

Olivia presented us to her guests—about fifteen people—all of whom turned their focus to the lamb cake. I deftly parried each and every jab about my baking until Olivia mercifully removed the cake to the kitchen where it would be free from ridicule until dessert.

"Looks like you could use one of these," Adam said, appearing out of nowhere with two martini glasses full of a pink concoction, garnished with the leaf of a daylily.

"What is it?"

"Olivia's secret recipe. You can even eat the flower. Ha! Hi, I'm Adam," he gushed, handing the second glass to Jeffers.

"It's nice to meet you," Jeffers said.

"Give it a minute," Adam said, laughing at himself before launching into a recitation about how legendary these parties of Olivia's were and how thrilled he was to have gotten an invite this time around.

Adam loved to dish and as long as he had one attentive listener, he could go on for hours. I took on the role of the devotee which gave Jeffers time to do a quick visual reconnaissance. In my periphery, I saw Jeffers' back stiffen. Then he planted himself firmly in front of Adam and gave him his undivided attention while I took advantage of our switch in roles to seek out what it was that had caught Jeffers' interest. It sought me out instead.

CHAPTER 20

"Well, hello, Detective," Shelagh Worthy chirped, appearing alongside us with a plate of hors d'oeuvres.

"Mrs. Worthy," Jeffers said, turning up the charm, "it's lovely to see you again."

Olivia was close by, refilling glasses from a pitcher of her secret cocktail.

"You two know each other?" Olivia asked her longtime friend.

"Why, yes," Shelagh said. "The detective here was out at our place a little while back, isn't that right? A string of robberies, if memory serves."

There was nothing in her manner that would suggest there was anything more to the story she was spinning, but Jeffers and I knew otherwise. And so did Shelagh.

"What a coincidence. Andre is a friend of Bella's," Olivia said by way of introducing me. "Bella, this is my dear friend Shelagh Worthy."

"I'm a big fan," Shelagh said, smiling in my direction, never hinting that we, too, were already acquainted.

"I had no idea you were a detective," Olivia said. "How exciting!"

"Not really. I mainly work the small stuff," Jeffers lied. "Street crimes, break and enters, that kind of thing."

Olivia and Adam were both clearly impressed. Adam, I could understand but Olivia's reaction was puzzling. I'd think a murderer having a police officer as a dinner guest would elicit a response that veered more toward the uneasy. But then again, she wasn't the sweetheart of the Canadian stage for nothing.

"I also work domestic abuse cases," Jeffers tacked on, much to my surprise.

There was nothing of note in Olivia's reaction. On the other hand, Shelagh Worthy's smile faltered ever so slightly.

"Would anybody care for an hors d'oeuvre?" she said. "I highly recommend the goat cheese croustade."

Adam followed her suggestion. I opted for a smoked salmon pinwheel type thing. Jeffers passed.

"Now, if you'll excuse me," she twittered and moved off to serve another part of the room. Olivia went to check on the dinner, followed by Adam who offered his help, leaving Jeffers and me alone with our nerves.

"Never even occurred to me that she'd be here," Jeffers said, referring to Shelagh.

"Me neither."

While it was clear Shelagh had never mentioned our visit to Olivia, the fact that she knew we had been sniffing around the details of Olivia's attack put us at risk. She would be watching us tonight.

"Did you happen to notice her reaction when you mentioned working Domestic Abuse?"

"Sure did," Jeffers said.

"What do think that's about?"

"Could have been afraid I was going to bring up Olivia's beating. Could have been something else."

"Like?"

"Like maybe she's had some experience of her own."

"Duck."

Jeffers shrugged.

I thought back to my phone conversation with Shelagh. Right before she hung up, she'd said Duck would be furious if he knew she was talking to me about Olivia. She was afraid. I also flashed back to the moment in our conversation when her tone changed, albeit so briefly. She had been talking about how much she'd envied Duck and Olivia's relationship. At the time I couldn't explain it, but it seemed to me now that it was a case of "be careful what you wish for."

Olivia was radiant as she held court at the head of the table. Even Peter's irritating attempts at wit could not distract. The speech she made before the meal about new beginnings and re-awakening was emotional, grateful, and so completely heartfelt that I almost forgot this little celebration was also a testament to a life taken away.

I turned my gaze on Peter Wynn, leaning back in his chair with his arms crossed. The corners of his mouth were raised in what appeared to be admiration of his ex-wife, but his eyes were downcast. I sensed a mourning of sorts. Like somehow Olivia's new chance at life had robbed him of something. I added Peter to the list of people with whom to have a follow-up conversation.

The other person on that list was Duck Worthy. He was absent from the festivities, so I turned my attention to his wife. Shelagh Worthy sat upright at Olivia's right hand. Shelagh's gaze never wavered from her friend. She looked at Olivia with the pride one might bestow upon one's own child, hanging on every word, and when Olivia finished, Shelagh enthusiastically began the inevitable applause.

"As soon as everyone starts eating, I'm going to do a little search of the upstairs," Jeffers whispered in my ear.

"Really?"

"Everyone will be occupied," Jeffers said. "Less chance of me getting caught rifling through Olivia's underwear drawer," he added with his trademark wink.

I rolled my eyes at his sense of humor, but couldn't help but agree that the timing made sense.

"Give me a little bit of everything. Especially the ham," he said. "I won't be long."

As soon as the applause died down and the serving dishes started circulating, Jeffers excused himself from the table, asked Olivia for directions to the bathroom, and left the room.

Conversation at the table turned to epicurean moans and compliments to the chef. As I suspected, Shelagh Worthy had played a large part in the creation of the feast, and Olivia made sure she shared in the accolades. Peter Wynn's praise of the meal came with derogatory undertones and earned him groans from the rest of the party and a playful slap on the arm from Shelagh. I watched the ease of the three of them, Olivia, Peter, and Shelagh. There was a lot of history at that end of the table, not all of it good, but history all the same. And history binds whether we like it or not.

I noticed Shelagh's gaze fall on Jeffers' empty chair. She took a quick survey of the room and was in the midst of sliding her chair away from the table when Jeffers returned. He bent over Olivia, whispering something to her that she clearly found amusing, and which, much to my relief, seemed to appease Shelagh as well.

"Well?" I asked when Jeffers had resumed his seat.

"Not much, I'm afraid," he said, before filling his mouth with a generous forkful of maple baked ham.

"Not much or nothing?" I asked quietly, knowing how risky this conversation was but too impatient to wait.

"Not much," he said with a smile.

I found myself in the kitchen, scraping dishes with Shelagh Worthy, when the meal had ended.

"I'm sorry your husband wasn't able to join us," I started

carefully. I was nervous and she knew it and she looked at me for several seconds before answering.

"As I told you on the phone, things between my husband and Olivia did not end easily. It would be extremely painful for them to see one another again."

"And he doesn't mind that you and Olivia have remained friends? I'm sorry. I know this is really none of my business—"

"No, it most certainly is not."

"It's just that I find it . . . odd . . . that your husband would have married his ex-wife's best friend. And that Olivia would be fine with it, too."

She scoffed.

I was on dangerous ground and was running out of time. "I mean, if their past is so difficult for your husband and Olivia to deal with, then aren't you a constant reminder?"

"You've got some nerve," she said. "Olivia and Duck have been my best friends since childhood. It's not in my being to turn my back on either one of them. However *odd* our relationship might be to you, we've made it work for over thirty years. And that's all you need to know."

"Have you ever known Duck to be violent?" I said as she turned to go.

She stopped momentarily, then made her way out of the kitchen without so much as a look back.

As we drove back to my place, I told Jeffers of my conversation with Shelagh.

"You either hit a nerve, or the idea of Duck raising a hand to her is so outlandish she couldn't dignify it with a response."

"So we're still no further ahead," I said.

"I wouldn't say that." He reached into his pocket and dropped a small blue pill into my hand. "That's my 'not much.' I found a bunch of pill bottles in the medicine cabinet. Nothing too unusual. Sleeping aids, migraine relief, but there was also a prescription for Celexa Oral."

"What's that?"

"An antidepressant."

"You just happen to know that?"

"Narcotics rotation at the Academy."

"Okay," I said, fingering the blue pill. The idea that Olivia took antidepressants was not surprising. "So what?"

"Celexa Oral comes in many colors: white, orange, terracotta. Never blue."

"Maybe she's using an old bottle. Maybe this is a simple ibuprofen or something."

"Maybe. But I thought I'd send it to the lab to have it checked out. Depending on how busy they are, I should be able to get the results by tomorrow afternoon."

"Great," I said, doubting the pill's significance. "What about the meantime?"

"I'm a man of my word, Samuel. We go to the Inspector."

CHAPTER 21

Skip Raines stood by the Inspector's desk, looking like a house had just fallen on his sister. Equal parts bewildered and enraged. Inspector Roger Morris had called him in after Jeffers and I had given him a full report of our discoveries. As Jeffers repeated our story for Raines' benefit, I watched the color rise in his face and marveled that a human being should be able to turn such a shade of purple without steam blowing out of his ears. Jeffers hadn't even gotten to the part about the bones being Olivia's.

Unlike Raines, Morris had shown little emotion during our tale. Nor had he spoken a word when we finished, except to call for Raines. He was not at all what I'd expected. The actor who played the Inspector on *Port Authority* had been well over six feet with shoulders that easily filled a size forty-six sports jacket. His physical power equaled the authority of the character and made him a force to be reckoned with. Roger Morris was a wiry little man. Gangly limbs on a scrawny frame. A few fine dark hairs seemed to be fighting off the grey that had overtaken most of what remained on his head, which was parted on the left and combed smooth. His nose, long and pointed, rested on top of a perfectly trimmed salt-and-pepper mustache and supported a pair of wire-rimmed glasses that were set low enough on the bridge so that he could look at you from over top of them with his close-set eyes. He sat with his elbows propped on his desk and his hands clasped together, index fingers extended and resting against a pair of pursed lips. He listened intently to Jeffers as if it were his first time hearing the information.

A scoff from Raines brought an end to my scrutiny of Morris' physique.

"The dental records," Jeffers said, raising his voice to be heard over Raines' outburst.

"I don't give a rat's ass," Raines said on top of Jeffers' remarks.

Both men were talking at once, neither one listening to the other, and both hell-bent on being heard. When the volume made their words incomprehensible, Morris raised one of his hands in an effortless gesture. Instantly, the shouting stopped.

"Please let him finish," Morris said softly, taking up his previous contemplative position and signaling to Jeffers with a nod of his head.

Raines pouted in his corner of the ring. I kept my eyes lowered so as not to attract any attention.

Jeffers found his calm and continued. As he relayed the details of the living Olivia's real identity as Marjorie Adelman, I sneaked a peak at Raines. The more Jeffers talked, the faster the color seemed to drain from his face. When Jeffers finished, Raines looked like he was about to be sick and made a move to excuse himself. Morris cleared his throat and Raines resumed his place, blotting the beads of sweat that had formed on his forehead. We all waited silently while Morris sifted through the pages Jeffers and I had included as part of our presentation.

"You'll want to look at these," Morris said finally, handing the file to Raines.

"Yes, sir," Raines managed.

Morris sighed and looked at Jeffers over the rims of his glasses. I held my breath. If Jeffers was going to be reprimanded, it would be now.

"Staff Sergeant Raines," Morris started, never taking his eyes off Jeffers, "I understand you were in charge of this case."

"Yes, sir."

"I seem to recall signing off on the paperwork and the case being closed."

"Yes, sir."

"It would now seem the situation is otherwise, wouldn't you agree?"

Morris took his gaze off Jeffers and looked at Raines. Raines fumbled to find his decorum and muttered something I couldn't make out but that seemed to satisfy Morris.

"I'd like Sergeant Jeffers to continue his investigation. Your support, Staff Sergeant, goes without saying."

Jeffers was staring at Morris with wide eyes and an even wider mouth. Raines looked like whatever he had had for breakfast was on its way up.

"But quietly, Sergeant Jeffers," Morris continued. "You are on the verge of making some very serious accusations here and, before you do, you must have proof to back up your allegations. Do you understand?"

"Yes, sir."

"What you are touching upon is going to affect many lives and I don't want even one of them turned upside down unless you are absolutely certain."

"I promise to be discreet, sir."

"Staff Sergeant, I'd like to review your notes from the Olivia Childries attack before you hand them over to Sergeant Jeffers."

Raines looked like he'd just received a kick to the stomach.

"I know they're more than thirty years old," Morris said, "but I trust you know where they are. I'll expect them on my desk first thing in the morning."

"Of course," Raines muttered then added a quick, "sir."

"And call the morgue. I don't want anything to happen to those remains until this whole mess is figured out. Do you understand?"

"Yes, sir."

"That's all."

Raines flew out of the room. Jeffers and I exchanged a look.

"Ms. James, thank you," Morris said, and I realized I was being dismissed as well.

Jeffers and I rose to go.

"Sergeant Jeffers, have a seat. We're not quite through."

By the time I arrived at the theatre for my matinee, I had still not heard from Jeffers. It had been two and a half hours since I'd closed the door of the Inspector's office. Given that Morris had okayed the investigation, I felt reasonably certain Jeffers wouldn't lose his place on the force. However, that did not guarantee his position within Major Crimes was secure once the investigation was over, or that he wouldn't face some kind of disciplinary action. Regardless of what he and I had uncovered, Jeffers had acted without authorization. Plus, he had jumped the line by taking our findings to the Inspector rather than his Staff Sergeant. Whatever reprimand Morris handed down would not be nearly as harsh as the one Jeffers could expect from Raines.

A knock on my dressing room door interrupted my transformation into Barbara. I had finished my makeup and was sitting in my corset and petticoat, about to put on my wig.

The stage manager tucked her bespectacled face around my door. "We're on a hold," she said in her apologetic way. "There's an accident on the highway and a couple of the buses are delayed."

The performance was a student matinee, and a late start was par for the course. School buses always seemed to be delayed for one reason or another and the chaos of hundreds of high-school-aged students converging on the same place at the same time was never as organized in actuality as it was in theory.

Caitlin left my room under a cloud of worry. I stood in the doorway and stared after her.

"What's the matter, Bella?"

I turned to find Olivia. Now that things were on the record with the police, Olivia was officially a person of interest. Whether she knew it or not. Morris had instructed Jeffers to be discreet in his investigation, but I knew it was only a matter of time before she got wind of what was going on. And of my involvement. If I had any hope of getting any more information out of her, I had to pretend today was a day like any other. And hope she bought it.

I gestured toward our stage manager's elfin form. For a moment Olivia and I watched as she delivered her message to Jarod Riley.

"Oh, that girl," Olivia said. "She really is the sweetest thing and very good at her job, but, my goodness, a person needs an antidepressant after having a conversation with her." Olivia chuckled, gave me a friendly squeeze, and disappeared down the hall into the wig room.

As if on cue, my cell phone rang. Jeffers. "I got the results from the lab," he said. "I was right. Those pills I found at Olivia's aren't antidepressants. For the most part they're a combination of baking powder and baking soda."

"Are you saying they're some kind of placebo?"

"I said 'for the most part.' The lab found small traces of Lopressor."

"What's that?"

"It's a beta-blocker. Typically used in treating patients with some form of heart disease."

Nothing I had ever read or heard about Olivia Childries alluded to her having suffered from any kind of heart condition. But then again, we weren't really dealing with Olivia Childries.

"Was there anything in Marjorie Adelman's history that

mentioned any kind of heart ailment?" I asked. "Perhaps this is all part of the cover. If Marjorie was being treated for heart disease, she would have to undergo her treatment in secret lest she be exposed. It would make sense that she would try to disguise her medication."

"My thoughts exactly," Jeffers said. "I'm on my way to Mercy Lodge to see if I can take a look at her medical records. Nancy Allenby may not be able to give me any info on Marjorie's whereabouts, but I'm hoping she's a little less rigid about her medical history."

"Good luck," I said. "What tale are you going to spin this time?"

"I haven't quite worked that out yet."

We shared an awkward pause. I was dying to know what had happened with the Inspector.

"Jeffers, how did everything go after I left Morris' office?"

I heard him inhale deeply. "Come for dinner tonight. I'll text you the address. Bring Moustache."

"Jeffers, is everything—"

A click told me he'd hung up. I sank into my dressing room chair as Caitlin's voice came over the intercom, announcing that the show would begin in ten minutes. Whatever had happened between Jeffers and Inspector Morris would have to wait. Out in the hall I could hear the chatter of students as the monitors that transmitted the sound throughout the backstage area crackled to life. One never knew what to expect from a student audience, but I was grateful I could focus on Barbara's drama rather than my own.

CHAPTER 22

"He stopped the show?" Aria Jeffers asked me wide-eyed.

I'd been telling her and Jeffers about the student matinee and how, in response to some of the students throwing pennies on the stage, the actor playing my father stopped mid-line and addressed the audience.

"He thanked the students for their generous offerings but assured them that the Shaw Festival pays all of its actors quite well and there was no need for any further contributions."

We all shared a laugh as Jeffers took his hand away from where he had been scratching Moustache's ears to refill my wine glass. Moustache pawed at Jeffers' leg.

"Did they stop?" Aria asked.

"Eventually," I said.

"Did he get in trouble?"

"Oh, no. He's been in the company for years. He was even married to the artistic director at one time. On top of that, he's an excellent actor. I think he got more offers to be taken out for a drink rather than anything remotely resembling a slap on the wrist."

"Speaking of slaps on the wrist," Jeffers said.

Aria took this as her cue to clear the salad plates and put the finishing touches on the main course. Moustache followed.

"My move to Major Crimes has been put on hold once this case wraps."

"I thought you were on probation anyway," I said. "You said

something about a six-month trial period before officially becoming a part of Major Crimes."

"True. I guess, then, my hold is on hold."

"What does that mean?"

"It means the Inspector thinks I know my stuff and wants me to conclude this case, but I've shown a shoddy attitude with regard to all the policies we have to follow, which can't be overlooked." Jeffers sighed. "He's right. I acted without any jurisdiction, broke the chain of command, stole police files, and I involved a civilian. Under the Police Act, I could be charged for any one of those. Imagine all of them!" Jeffers held his head in his hands. "When . . . *if* I close this investigation, I'll be suspended and there will be a divisional review."

"How long will that take?"

"Six months. A year. Who knows? The last case took three years."

"And after that?"

Jeffers offered up his familiar grin. "That depends on the Superintendent."

"All the way to the top, huh?"

"Not all the way. Thank goodness. Chief Ambrose is a real ball buster," he said, referring to the NRP's Chief of Police. "No, it goes to a man named Mitchell. He's fair. I've always liked him. He was my unit commander at the B.E.U for a time. He knows what kind of cop I am, so I hope that works in my favor."

"I think if they were going to kick you off the job they would have done it," Aria said, entering the dining room with a steaming platter of Moroccan spiced chicken and Moustache trotting hopefully at her heels.

"I agree," I said. "Clearly the Inspector is impressed by what you've managed to uncover, regardless of how you did it. And, yes, he has to follow procedure, otherwise every cop will think they can do whatever they want with no consequences. You might get suspended but, at the same time, it all might get swept under the rug because you did a great investigation. Even if they transfer you to another unit, there's no way they're going to let you go."

"As long as it's not back to B.E.U.," Aria said, doling out generous portions of chicken, couscous, vegetables, and apricots.

Jeffers rolled his eyes playfully, then reached out and touched his wife's hand. "If it makes you feel better, I've heard they might be disbanding that unit."

"Really? Why?" Aria dropped some couscous onto the floor in her excitement. Moustache, ever the perfect guest, was only too happy to take care of the cleanup.

"I don't know and it doesn't really matter. What matters is this case. Right now."

I had to hand it to him. Whether for my benefit or his wife's, Jeffers refused to nurse the bruises he had received earlier in the day. He refused to behave like a man whose career was on the line, but rather like the dedicated detective he had come to be. I looked to Aria who was resolute in her support of her husband. The two of them were a formidable team and I realized if I wanted to play in their game, I had to reject all thoughts of possible defeat.

"So where does that leave me?" I asked.

"Detective Samuel," Jeffers said, leaning over the table and tapping me lightly on each shoulder with his dinner knife, "I hereby deputize you into the ranks of the Niagara Regional Police."

"You can't do that," I said and laughed. "First of all, you're no sheriff and, secondly, I don't even think deputizing is a real thing in Canada. Is it?"

"Aw, come on. I even got you this," he said, reaching into his pocket and handing me a small paper bag before settling back in his chair with a smug grin.

"Ha," I said, pulling out a plastic toy sheriff's badge. "Cute."

Jeffers laughed. So did Aria. Moustache was immediately at my side to sniff the starred badge and determine its edibility.

"Okay," I said. "All kidding aside. I'm serious. I want to be involved."

"I'm serious, too." Jeffers handed me a folded piece of paper. "This is a dispensation from the Inspector, giving you formal authorization to continue working on the investigation. As a consultant. You know Olivia and theatre business, so it makes sense."

My jaw dropped.

"You have to be extra careful, though," Jeffers said. "It's more than my career on the line if anything happens to you. Inspector Morris may have given you special consideration, but you are not protected by the system the way police officers are. You have no special authority where the law is concerned."

I nodded and took a moment to read the paper. I thought about the real Olivia and felt more determined than ever to get her the justice she deserved.

"Can I still wear the badge?" I asked, to which Aria giggled and Jeffers replied by throwing an apricot at me from across the table.

"I wish she would let me help," I said to Jeffers. We were making ourselves comfortable in his living room while his pregnant wife cleared the table and ran water for the dinner dishes.

"Now that we have the support of the department behind this investigation, she's not going to let anything get in the way of me closing this case. Not even dishes. Besides, she's got Moustache."

"*He's* the one doing the dishes."

"Aria's so certain that if I can catch the bad guy, or gal in this case, the superintendent will overlook all of my offenses and give me a commendation instead." He gave a wry laugh, the first time this whole evening he gave so much as a hint of defeat.

"You'd better hope the baby looks like her," I said, changing the subject and, hopefully, lightening it up.

"Don't I know it!"

Aria Jeffers might have been six months pregnant, but the only thing giving that away was a small, perfect bump in her belly. Otherwise, she was in fantastic shape and I doubted she had gained more than a couple of extra pounds. Everything about Aria was petite, from her waistline to her stature. She stood to Jeffers' shoulder, which made her about five-feet-three. Her white blonde hair was cut in a long bob that fell just below a slightly angular jaw, with layers that kissed her high cheekbones. She was pretty in the way the typical television version of a high-school cheerleader is pretty. The girl-next-door type that every mother hopes her son will bring home. But she had warmth and depth and a face that expressed exactly how she felt. I could tell when she looked at Jeffers how deep her love for him went. It was the same look Jeffers had on his face when he looked at her. I felt the pangs of envy and shook them off.

"So, boss, what did you learn from your trip to Mercy Lodge?" I asked.

"Nothing. Medical history was clean. No history of heart disease of any kind. Not even a murmur."

"Then why would she be taking Lopressor?"

"No idea. I have the lab running more tests. Maybe they missed something. First thing tomorrow I'm going to take a look at Raines' notes from the night of the attack. I have a feeling there were a lot of questions that weren't asked, especially of the people who might have been involved."

"Duck Worthy?"

"For starters. I think another trip to Coldwater might be in order. I'm also interested in Peter Wynn."

"You think Peter could have been working with Marjorie?"

"Possibly."

"What would his motive be?"

"I don't know. Shelagh Worthy said Duck walked in on Peter and Olivia having sex. What if it wasn't Olivia?"

"What if it was Marjorie? If Peter and Marjorie were together before the attack that would certainly explain his quick marriage to the new 'Olivia.' But not why they would have to kill the real Olivia in order to be together."

"Marjorie was trying to escape her abusive ex-husband and start a new life. She couldn't very well ask him for a divorce. Not without letting him in on her whereabouts."

"True. So, since we've already determined there's nothing to suggest a connection between Marjorie and Olivia, the connection has to come from Marjorie's accomplice, and that accomplice has to be one of the two men in Olivia's life."

"We need to figure out which one."

"Let's hope this time around they feel like talking."

"It's an official police investigation now," Jeffers said. "They don't really have a choice."

CHAPTER 23

I was in the middle of a costume fitting for *The Hothouse* when I was paged over the theatre's intercom to sign for a delivery at the stage door.

"You're going to have to go like this," the designer said with a groan.

I looked at myself in the mirror. According to the drawings, the dress would be a sexy, below the knee, cobalt blue pencil dress with a mock turtleneck and three-quarter length sleeves accented by a thin black belt. At the moment, however, the material was pinned together within an inch of its life and looked more like a home-ec. project gone wrong.

The fitting rooms were located up a flight of stairs from where my delivery was waiting, and in order to avoid sticking myself with any of the hundreds of pins that held my dress together, I took the steps one at a time with as straight a leg as possible. When I'd reached the fourth stair from the bottom, I could see that my messenger was not alone in the small lobby area. Manda Rogers was chatting to Deanna, the receptionist, with Dr. Gorgeous by her side. I contemplated a quick getaway, but after one leg lift, I knew that negotiating the pins while climbing was going to be far less graceful than coming down. If Dr. Gorgeous had to see me in this state, it was better to be on the descent. To make matters worse, Manda looked radiant.

She laughed at something Deanna said and flipped her hair as she turned to share the joke with Dr. Gorgeous. On the way, her eyes met mine and she said, "Is this a new fashion trend?"

"Straight from Milan," I said, meeting her sarcasm with wit.

Thankfully, Dr. Gorgeous added a complimentary chuckle to the exchange. Manda gave him a sideways glance before training the crosshairs back on me. I steadied myself for her retort, which was cut short by Isaac Dunphy, the stage manager for the musical, nearly trampling me as he flew down the stairs. An iron grip on the railing was the only thing that kept me upright.

"Manda, what's taking so long?" he asked, breathless. "Oh," he said, noticing Dr. Gorgeous, "are you the vet?"

"Yes."

"Oh, thank God. Follow me."

Without waiting to see if the doctor followed, Isaac dashed up the stairs as quickly as he had come down. Dr. Gorgeous followed, offering a dreamy "Nice to see you" as he passed me. I smiled like a smitten fool, only to have it wiped from my face as Manda went by me, a little closer than necessary, ensuring that several of the pins made contact with my skin. I winced.

"Oh, be careful," Manda said. "If you get blood on that, the designer will kill you."

I shuffled down the remaining stairs and looked to Mr. Canada Post. "Hi. You have a delivery for me?"

"Campbell James?"

"Yep."

"Registered Mail. Here you go," he said, offering me an electronic signature pad before handing me the envelope.

When Mr. Canada Post had gone, I turned to Deanna and said, "What was that all about? Why did Isaac need a vet?"

"One of the lambs in the musical fell into the orchestra pit."

"Is it all right?"

She looked at me as if I had spoken in a different language and then shrugged.

I resumed the daunting task of mounting the staircase while

wondering why theatres still think it's revolutionary to feature live animals on stage. At the same time, my insides were enjoying a momentary rejoicing upon learning that Dr. Gorgeous was, in fact, there on official business rather than the pleasure I had initially assumed.

It wasn't until I had been liberated from my costume and returned to my dressing room that I looked carefully at the envelope. The return address indicated a Prince Edward Island law firm. Breaking the seal, I pulled out a letter-headed document offering me condolences on the passing on my grandmother and notifying me that her estate had been settled. As her sole beneficiary, I was entitled to the enclosed inheritance. Puzzled, I reached back into the official envelope and pulled out a check for an amount that nearly made my heart stop. Seconds later, I was on my cell phone. Marie Coombs answered on the fourth ring.

"Marie, it's Bella James."

"Campbell, how nice to hear from you."

"Marie, I just received a check from Terri-Mae's estate. I thought I had been clear that whatever was left over after expenses should be shared among you and Terri-Mae's friends and the church."

"I know what you said, Bella. Joe took a very fair fee for handling your grandmother's legal matters. As for the rest, we're all in agreement."

"Who's 'we'? *I'm* the beneficiary so *I* should be the one to say where the money goes."

"Campbell, calm down. Terri-Mae saved that money for you. So you'd be taken care of. All of us here know that. She was very proud of what she was able to put away. She promised your father on his deathbed that she would look out for you until the day she died and whether you like it or not, this is her way of doing that."

The lump in my throat and the welling in my eyes each competed for attention.

"You know I don't deserve this," I said.

"Campbell, sweetheart, don't you think we all knew how difficult things were for you growing up?"

"I was awful," I said, giving in to my tears.

"Now you listen to me," she said. "You were no more awful than any typical teenager who thinks she rules the world, or my own grandchildren for that matter. And they don't have half the excuse for acting out that you did. I don't know if she ever told you, but your father was no saint when he was a boy. We all got down on our knees and gave thanks when he finally grew into the man he was."

I laughed. Marie joined me.

"But I grew up, too, Marie, and I still wasn't—"

"That's for the two of you to work out when it's your time to meet again."

"It's a lot of money," I said.

"Yes, it is," Marie said proudly.

"I'd really like to do something for you and Joe. You handled everything! Isn't there somewhere you've always wanted to see or something you've always meant to do but haven't gotten around to it? Please let me do something good for once."

"Well," Marie said, "Joe and I have always talked about going on a cruise. Now that he's retired—"

"Great! Let me know where and when and I'll make the arrangements. And," I said, getting excited, "Terri-Mae's birthday is coming up, so I want you to take all the ladies you two played bridge with out for lobster. In her honor. Send me the bill." I heard Marie laughing. "And that cruise? You're going first class!"

★ ★ ★ ★ ★

"What are you going to do with the rest of it?" Natalie asked when I called her with the news.

"I have no idea. I have such mixed feelings about accepting it. I'll probably invest it until I can think of something better. If there is anything better."

"Bella, I think you should look at this as an opportunity to use the money in a way that would really please Terri-Mae. You're in a good place, financially, so you don't need it to live on. I think you need to think of something Terri-Mae always wanted to give you but couldn't because you wouldn't let her."

"Like what?"

"I'm not trying to start a fight here, Bel. I know how hard losing Terri-Mae has been on you. I'm just saying that it would be nice if you could use the money in a way that might have a deeper meaning. For both of you."

I was all too aware of my shortcomings and failings, and I knew Natalie was right. "Well, I don't have to decide anything today," I said.

"No," she agreed. "You'll figure it out."

Our conversation shifted to other topics—her work, Zack's latest art show, Austin's bout with diarrhea following an overindulgence of frozen veal Natalie had left to thaw on the counter. I masterfully deflected any attempts she made at discussing Jarod Riley and whether I had ever followed up on our one date. Without going into too much detail, I was about to update Natalie on the latest in the Olivia Childries saga when my call-waiting announced Jeffers.

"I should go anyway," Natalie said when I told her of the incoming call. "I have a student in an hour and should probably take Austin out for a 'cleansing' first."

We made plans to talk in the coming days and I switched over to Jeffers.

"You free tomorrow morning?" he asked.

"It depends," I said.

"Care to sit in on a little interview with Mr. Peter Wynn?"

"Would I?" I said, channeling my best Judy Garland/Mickey Rooney enthusiasm.

"Great. I'll pick you up at ten."

"Hey," I said, "did anything come from those notes Raines gave you?"

"Nothing that wasn't in the official report. It's weird, though, his notes were so neat."

"Why is that weird?"

"When you're taking notes at a crime scene, statements from witnesses and all that, there's no time to worry about penmanship. The important thing is to get down all the information as quickly as possible. That's why we have to write up reports, because our handwriting and shorthand is usually illegible to anyone but ourselves."

"And Raines' notes were too neat?"

"I had no trouble reading them is all I'm saying."

"Maybe," I said, at a bit of a loss, "it was one of his first cases and he was trying to be extra careful."

"Hmmm," Jeffers voiced, unconvinced. "Anyway, ten o'clock?"

"I'll see you then."

CHAPTER 24

"Wow!" Jeffers said as we pulled up in front of a very grand house on the prestigious Niagara Parkway.

The Parkway extended from Niagara-on-the-Lake to Niagara Falls and showcased some of the largest, most expensive homes in the area. Those on the lucky side of the road had spectacular views of the Niagara River and gorge. Peter Wynn was one of the lucky ones.

"I thought you said this guy was an agent," Jeffers said.

"He is," I said, "and one of the best, I hate to admit."

"I'm in the wrong business," Jeffers said and whistled.

While Peter did have an office in Toronto bearing his name, he preferred to work from home and let his staff have the office. Looking at the house, I wondered if it was the home he had shared with Olivia. It was extremely large but not nearly as grandiose as I had imagined. For a man who loved to flaunt his wealth at every turn, his residence looked surprisingly tasteful.

The same could not be said for the robe Peter was wearing when he opened the door. If it had been made from spun gold, it couldn't have looked any more ostentatious.

"Mr. Wynn. It's very nice to see you again. Thank you so much for your cooperation," Jeffers said, extending his hand.

"What's *she* doing here?" Peter asked.

"Ms. James has been asked to consult on this case."

"Why? Because she once played a cop on TV?" Peter snickered.

"He's just mad he didn't get the commission," I said to Jeffers, meeting Peter's narrow gaze and matching his arrogant smile with one of my most charming.

"Inspector Morris believes that Ms. James has invaluable insight to lend to this case and has asked for her involvement personally," Jeffers said. "I trust we don't have a problem?"

"Of course not," Peter said and invited us inside. "I've been trying to get Bella to my house for years," he added with a wink.

He led us into a sunken living room and motioned for us to sit on a caramel colored suede settee. He sat on its twin across from us, his back to a wall of windows that offered a panoramic view of the gorge and of the neighboring United States.

"So what's all this about?" he asked.

"You're aware that human remains were discovered on Ms. James' property?"

Peter nodded his pompous head and smiled, as if he knew where this was going.

"We have reason to believe those remains are connected to the night Olivia Childries was attacked and we'd like to ask you a few questions."

"This is preposterous!" Peter said. "That was over thirty years ago. How am I supposed to—"

"Yes, it was over thirty years ago," Jeffers interrupted, "and we understand you were with Ms. Childries shortly before her attack. Can you tell us about that?"

Peter fired a look at me. "This is absurd," he protested and made a move to stand.

"Perhaps I can jog your memory," Jeffers said. "Duck Worthy mentioned walking in on you and Ms. Childries engaging in sexual—"

"That's enough!" Peter bellowed, reaching his full height.

"Mr. Wynn," Jeffers said calmly, "you can answer our questions here or down at the station. Either way, you are going to answer them. You can choose the venue."

I couldn't understand where Peter's indignation was coming from. In my opinion, there was no need for him to be so defensive. Even if it had been clandestine at the time, Peter and Olivia married so soon after her divorce from Duck. Tongues would have wagged about an affair. Shelagh Worthy had known of it. Others probably had, too. Peter's ire made little sense.

Eventually, he resumed his seat. "I don't know anything about any bones," he said. "Or who attacked Olivia."

Jeffers said, "Can you tell us how long you and Ms. Childries were having an affair?"

"What does that have to do with anything?"

"Mr. Wynn, please answer the question."

"I don't have to talk to you," Peter said, obviously trying to buy time.

"You're not under arrest," Jeffers said. "However, if you'd feel more comfortable with a lawyer present . . ."

Whether he felt that a lawyer equaled some kind of admission of guilt, I didn't know, but he waved off the suggestion with an irritated flick of his hand, then sank into the settee with his head in his hands.

"She called me," he said, after a lengthy pause.

"Ms. Childries?"

Peter nodded. "She called me and asked me to come over."

"When was this?"

"Around four, I guess."

"Did she say what she wanted?"

"No, just asked if I could come by right away."

I opened my mouth to say something, but Jeffers touched his index finger to his lips, then aimed the same finger in Peter's direction.

"When I got there, she was in her robe," Peter continued. "It was like she'd been drugged or something."

"What do you mean," I asked.

"She was out of it. Incoherent. There were flowers everywhere. And champagne. I thought maybe she was drunk but . . . it was more than that."

"Did she say anything to you?" Jeffers asked.

"I don't think she recognized me."

"What happened next?"

Eyes still averted, Peter's shoulders slumped. "I managed to grab hold of her right before she passed out. I brought her to her bedroom so she could lie down and . . ." Peter started to cry. "I loved her."

Tears streamed down his cheeks. "I loved her so much, but her heart was with Duck." He inhaled deeply and seemed to gather some strength. "I put her to bed and while I was doing it, her robe shifted slightly and I could see . . . God, she was so beautiful. Before I realized what I was doing, I had undone the sash. I had loved her for so long and here she was in front of me. Beautiful. And I was able to finally touch her and kiss her and—"

"Oh my God," I whispered.

"When Duck Worthy walked in on you," Jeffers said, "you were in the middle of raping his wife?"

Peter, who'd been sobbing, let out a howl. Then he said, "I didn't even know Duck had been there. I found out later that night at the hospital. When . . . when I had finished, I was so ashamed at what I'd done. I dressed her, tucked her in and left."

His eyes met ours for the first time. As if he was appealing to us for mercy. Then, wiping his face on the sleeve of his robe, he sniffled and said, "After she was attacked, she didn't have any memory of what had happened. Not of the attack. Or what I'd done. Duck confronted me at the hospital. Assumed Olivia and

I had been having an affair. I went along with it."

Jeffers gave Peter a chance to settle before pressing forward with why we were there.

"Mr. Wynn, are you absolutely sure the woman you were with that night was Olivia Childries?"

"What? Of course it was Olivia! Who else would it have been?"

Jeffers didn't answer but instead asked, "What can you tell us about your marriage to Ms. Childries?"

Taken aback by the question, Peter turned his gaze on me and said, "I know you think I'm a louse."

I thought that was too favorable a description but I kept my opinion to myself and averted my eyes.

"You have no idea what Olivia went through afterwards," he said. "On top of having to endure surgery after surgery, she had no memory of her life. Her friend Shelagh sat with her every day, going through old photo albums and telling her stories of their childhood. Nothing registered, but she seemed to really want to know the person she once was. She worked so hard so she could be that person again. She didn't want anyone to know how bad things were. I came every day with newspaper clippings and reviews and we would talk about theatre and her triumphs." His eyes started to well up again. "Her recovery took years. And I was by her side for all of it. Because I had loved her and, yes, because I felt guilty! Do you have any idea how responsible I felt? If I hadn't done what I did, Duck Worthy would have come home as usual and the monster that attacked her never would have found her alone."

I didn't point out that Duck might have attacked Olivia because he believed she'd had an affair. Either way, Peter would have been inadvertently responsible and I didn't think he'd be able to handle any more guilt.

"She asked me once if I was hanging around out of pity," Peter continued. "To prove I was sincere, I proposed. Never expected her to say yes."

"Would you say you had a good marriage?" Jeffers asked.

"We had a lot of good times. And we had some not very good times. She was never quite the same after the assault. Personally. Professionally. She needed to relearn so much. God, she even needed to learn how to speak again because her jaw had been . . . her first few shows were appalling, if you must know. Not her fault, of course. And no one would ever dare admit it. We got her a coach and, eventually, she found her legs. Got her rhythm back, and look at her now."

"And personally?" I asked

"What?"

"You said she was never the same professionally or personally."

"There's nothing I could ever put my finger on. She was missing something, you know? Whatever it was that made her Olivia. She seemed to have lost a part of that."

I looked at Jeffers wondering if he was going to inform this man who sat beaten and crumpled before us that the woman he had married was, in fact, not the woman he had loved.

Jeffers licked his bottom lip before resting his teeth on it. I sensed he was wondering the very same thing.

Finally, he said, "Mr. Wynn, does the name Marjorie Adelman mean anything to you?"

"No. Is that the woman who was buried in Bella's yard?"

"I'm sorry," Jeffers said, "I'm not at liberty to disclose any further details at the moment. Thank you for your time. You've been very helpful. We'll be in touch if there's anything further. We'll show ourselves out."

"Bella?" Peter called out as we made our way to the front door.

I turned to see him staring at me, his eyes pleading.

"I won't tell Olivia, if that's what you're worried about. It's not something she should hear from me," I said, leaving the great Peter Wynn to pick up the shattered pieces of himself that lay scattered on his designer rug.

CHAPTER 25

I had about an hour until I had to be at the theatre. Before parting, Jeffers and I had agreed that we would visit Duck Worthy the following day. Both of our heads were still in a fog after Peter Wynn's big reveal and neither of us seemed in the mood to discuss it further without giving the revelation some time to process.

Knowing there was no way I could put in an even passable performance with Peter's words still ringing in my ears, I decided the best way to clear my head was a brisk walk and some fresh air.

Moustache, clearly not expecting me home at this hour, was lounging on the bed upstairs. The thump of his feet hitting the floor gave him away. He stuck his tousled head around the bedroom door frame and looked down at me, question marks forming behind his eyes. His fur, flattened on the bottom of his face, made it appear as though he had no chin. I jangled his leash. He barreled down the stairs, leaping over the final two, and skidded to a halt in front of the door, where he jumped straight up in the air three times before settling himself on his plush bottom.

Together we burst into the day's brightness, him pulling at the leash, me laughing. It always amazed me how much sheer joy Moustache took in a simple thing like a walk around the neighborhood. I watched him negotiate the roads with his nose to the ground and a skip in his step, marveling at how oblivious he was to anything but the absolute perfection of the moment.

I decided to follow the dog's lead, literally and emotionally, and for the duration of our time together, allowed myself to let go of all thoughts of murder and rape and stolen identities. I surrendered to the warmth of the sun and the joy contained in a deep inhale of spring.

Erna Weins was on her hands and knees on her front lawn, a large paper yard-waste bag on the ground next to her. I smiled as Moustache and I passed and made some generic comment about the weather to which she responded with an equally generic comment. Moustache and I got a few more paces in before Erna called out, "They know what you're doing."

"Excuse me?" I said, turning to face her.

"You and your policeman. They know you've been asking questions about that night. You be careful," she said, getting to her feet and brushing some of the outdoors off the legs of her pants. "They're not happy about it."

For a moment I was so stunned it was all I could do to watch her amble up the path to her front door. Finally, my senses came back to life and I called out, "Erna? Who's 'they'?"

She continued her retreat into her house without looking back.

CHAPTER 26

"She knows something. Probably *everything*. I can't believe this!"

"I'm sorry, Bella," Jeffers said. "She didn't say anything she hasn't said before. Repeated her initial statement word for word."

After Erna's cryptic warning the day before, I had called Jeffers and asked him to follow up on it. Not only did Erna hold true to the story she had told the police thirty years ago, but she maintained that the conversation she and I had shared that afternoon had not extended beyond a mutual appreciation for a beautiful day.

"Someone must have threatened her or something," I said. "I mean why would she lie about this?"

Jeffers was silent.

"I didn't make it up," I said.

"I know that," he said, "but we can't very well haul a seventy-year-old woman down to the station and threaten to rip her fingernails out if she doesn't tell us the truth."

"That's not what was suggesting," I said, slapping him playfully on the arm and smiling for the first time in hours. We were en route to our second visit to Duck Worthy. "It's just that whatever she knows could blow this whole case wide open. If nothing else, it might have saved us this trip."

Jeffers made the final turn into the Worthys' driveway and parked his car alongside an idling Ford pickup.

"Looks like we got here just in time," he said, waving through the window to an irritated Duck Worthy.

"You here to waste my time about another made-up case?" Duck asked from the driver's seat of his truck as Jeffers and I got out of the car.

"No, sir." Jeffers flashed his badge. "I'm afraid we weren't properly introduced the last time. I'm Detective Serge—"

"I don't care what your name is. What do you want?"

Jeffers had planned to ease into the conversation, but Duck's hostility changed the game plan.

"The department has reopened your ex-wife's case and we'd like to ask you a few questions about the night she was attacked."

Duck clenched his jaw and stared hard at Jeffers. Eventually, he turned off the ignition but made no move to get out of his truck.

"Mr. Worthy, you might be more comfortable in your house or workshop."

"I'm fine."

"Well then, perhaps you can tell us what you remember from that night."

Duck heaved a heavy sigh. "I got home a little after five. There were candles lit. A bottle of champagne. House smelled of flowers. People were always sending Olivia congratulatory flowers." His last few syllables were barely audible and were spoken with fondness. "I . . . uh . . . heard some noise in the bedroom and figured Olivia had planned a romantic night."

"Can you tell us what happened next?"

"I think you already know."

"If you could please tell us what you saw."

Duck's grip tightened around the steering wheel and he shifted his gaze to look out the windshield. Then he rounded his angry gaze on us and said, "I saw Olivia in bed with her agent, all right?"

"Peter Wynn."

"Yes, damn it!"

"You said you got home just after five. Is that the time you normally got home or was that night different?"

"Got home the same time every night. Does it make a difference?"

I knew what Jeffers was thinking because I was thinking the same thing. Something about the timing didn't feel right and I guessed we'd revisit it later, when we were alone.

"What happened after you encountered your wife and Mr. Wynn?" Jeffers said.

"I left."

"Did you confront them at all?"

A slight shake of the head.

"Did they see you?"

"She had her eyes closed and he was—"

"And you're sure it was Olivia?"

"What kind of question is that?"

Jeffers let it go. "So, you just left?"

"I did."

"Where did you go?"

"I drove! I got in my car and just drove."

"Did anyone see you? Is there anyone who can account for your whereabouts after you left your house?"

"You've got to be kidding. Is that what this is all about? You think I had something to do with what happened to Livvie?"

"Mr. Worthy, we're just trying to—"

"Don't you 'Mr. Worthy' me!"

For a moment, emotion overtook Duck Worthy and for that moment we could see the man underneath the brawn and gruff exterior. A man who had loved deeply and who had never recovered from his wife's betrayal.

In a quiet voice, Duck finally said, "For God's sake, this happened over thirty years ago. Olivia didn't want it pursued then and I can't imagine what would have made her reconsider. So if you don't mind, there's somewhere I need to be."

Duck started his pickup and moved the gearshift into reverse.

Jeffers ran to the driver's side window as the truck began to move backward. "A woman was murdered that same night," he called out, "and we believe there's a connection."

"Who was murdered?" Duck asked, touching the brake.

Jeffers stood looking at Duck while I said, "I'm afraid, we're not at liberty to disclose that information."

It was inevitable that we'd eventually have to tell Duck about Olivia's murder, but that moment was not yet.

"Human remains were found on the property of the house you and Olivia were living in," I said. "Tests show the date of death coincides with the night of the attack. Whoever attacked your wife may have been responsible for this murder as well. We're trying to put the pieces together."

"If you'll give us just a few more minutes," Jeffers said, "you can be on your way."

Duck threw the Ford into Park but left the engine running.

"How did you hear about your wife's attack?" Jeffers asked.

"As I said, I was out driving. And no, I didn't see anyone. I got back to the house around nine. Didn't know what I was going to do, but knew I'd have to go home sooner or later. When I got there, the place was crawling with cops. They told me what had happened and I rushed to the hospital."

"The police report mentioned that you had a towel around your right hand."

Duck laughed. "Are you married, Detective?"

"I am."

"Do you love your wife?"

"More than anything."

"And if you walked in on the love of your life in bed with

another man?"

"I'd want to hit something."

"Right. And before you ask, it was the dashboard of my car that got the worst of it."

"What happened when you got to the hospital?"

Duck turned the keys in his idling truck, bringing the engine to a stop, and stepped out of the cab. "This is going to take more than a few minutes isn't it?" He leaned his bulk against the door and folded his sturdy arms across his chest.

Jeffers nodded.

"When I got there, Livvie was in surgery. Shelagh was distraught."

"Mrs. Worthy was at the hospital before you arrived?"

"I guess when the hospital couldn't reach me they called Olivia's next emergency contact, Shelagh."

"Can you tell me how Olivia seemed when she got out of surgery?"

"I never saw her," Duck said, crumpling under the weight of regret. "Well, that's not entirely true. I sat up with her all night. She was unconscious. I could barely recognize her. Shelagh finally convinced me to go home and get some sleep. Said I'd be no use to Livvie in the state I was in. Livvie woke up while I was gone and when I got back, Shelagh told me she said she didn't ever want to see me again. That she wanted a divorce." He paused. "Look, I don't really see what the end of my marriage has to do with anything. You said there was a murder?"

Jeffers and I knew the rest of the story so there really wasn't any need to continue with this line of questioning. We knew the woman in the hospital had been Marjorie Adelman. What we didn't know was whether or not Duck knew it, too.

"Do you know a Marjorie Adelman?" Jeffers asked.

Duck shook his head. There had been no flicker of recognition at the mention of the name. Nor had there been the prolonged hesitation or overly quick response that are signs of lying. Either Duck had been prepared for the question or he was telling the truth.

"What does she have to do with all this? Is she the one who was killed?" Duck asked.

"We believe she and another person may have been involved in Olivia's beating," Jeffers said. "And the murder."

"Do you know where she is? Have you talked to her?" Duck's questions took on a desperate air, like for the first time in three decades he might finally get some answers. And maybe even some closure.

"I'm afraid we can't—"

"Damn it, you come here and force me to relive the worst night of my life and you don't even have the decency to tell me what's going on! I've answered your questions. I've stood by while you have accused me of doing the unthinkable to the only woman I've ever loved. Screw you and your 'we're not at liberty to say' bullshit! I want you off my land!"

My instincts had been correct. Duck Worthy was no monster. He was a man who had lost the only thing that had ever mattered in his life without ever knowing why and had spent over thirty years trying to scrape out some kind of existence. My heart was breaking as I watched the walls Duck had spent years building up crumble all around him. I ached to reach out. To tell him that Olivia had never stopped loving him. To bring him some peace. But I knew the knowledge I had would cause a different kind of pain.

"Duck?" Shelagh's voice rang out from where she stood, peeking around the side door of their house. "Is everything okay?"

"Go inside, Shelagh."

"I heard yelling and I—"

"Good God, woman, go inside!" Duck bellowed before turning on Jeffers and me. "And if you're not off my property in ten seconds, I'll call the cops and have you arrested for trespassing! Ten . . ."

"Mr. Worthy, please," I began.

"Nine . . ."

"Mr. Worthy," I begged, "the remains that were found—"

"Eight!"

"The bones—"

"Seven!"

"The woman who was murdered—"

"Six!"

"It was Olivia!"

CHAPTER 27

Duck stopped counting and stared at me. Jeffers and I froze. I hadn't meant to blurt out that Olivia had been killed. It was not the way Jeffers and I had planned to break the news and it was certainly not the way I wanted Duck to hear it. But it was out there and the three of us stood motionless on the Worthy property, staring at one another.

"Mr. Worthy, I am so sorry," I said. "This is not the way we wanted to tell you. We had to know if you were involved before we could—"

"Stop talking." He sank to the ground and sat with his back against the side of his truck, his knees bent. "Let me get this straight. You're telling me the body found in the yard is—" His mouth formed the O that began Olivia's name, but he couldn't bring himself to utter it.

"I'm so sorry," Jeffers said.

Duck raised a hand. "And that she's been dead for all this time?"

Jeffers offered a sympathetic nod.

"Are you mad? I've seen her in the papers! Shelagh is her best friend! Do you know how crazy you sound?"

"Mr. Worthy," Jeffers interjected, "we believe a woman named Marjorie Adelman murdered Olivia and has been living as her ever since."

"You believe?"

"We know for a fact. We were able to match the dental records of the body that was found to those of Olivia's. She'd had some specific dental work done as a teenager."

"Her . . . her father gave her some kind of implant or something."

"That's right," Jeffers said. "The match was indisputable."

Duck let out a low moan as the reality started to sink in.

"We were also able to test the fingerprints of the woman claiming to be Olivia," Jeffers continued. "They matched Marjorie Adelman."

Duck's legs collapsed and he covered his face with his massive hands. His shoulders slumped and trembled. "The attack?" he asked from behind his hands.

"From what we've been able to piece together," I said as tactfully as I could, "Marjorie and an accomplice orchestrated the attack so she'd be able to reconstruct her face to look like Olivia's. The reconstruction would also help to explain any physical discrepancies to those who knew Olivia."

Duck looked up, his face stained with tears. "What kind of person does something like that?"

I shook my head. I knew Marjorie had been desperate to escape her ex-husband, but I hadn't yet been able to come to terms with the lengths she might have gone to in order to do so.

"What we haven't been able to uncover is how Marjorie knew Olivia," I said. "Why she chose her."

"My God," Duck Worthy whispered.

"If you know anything about Marjorie Adelman—anything at all—it could help us."

Duck shook his head. He sat, despondent, for quite some time before asking, "Was it Wynn?"

"At this time," Jeffers said, "we don't believe he was involved."

Jeffers and I looked at one another, neither of us wanting to be the bearer of even more ghastly news. In a wordless draw of straws, I pulled the short one.

As I relayed Peter's confession, Duck looked like he'd been punched.

"She didn't betray you," I said quickly, hoping it came as some relief. "She never stopped loving you."

I couldn't imagine what Duck must have been going through. To learn the truth after so much time.

"How did she die?" he asked.

"She was suffocated," Jeffers said. "At this time we don't know how."

"If I hadn't left . . ." Duck said to no one in particular.

"Mr. Worthy, please, you can't blame yourself."

"Oh my God, my God, my God," Duck repeated, rocking himself.

Jeffers caught my eye and indicated that we should probably go and leave Duck to grieve in private. We had only taken a few steps when Duck said, "I wish you could have known her. She was the most beautiful person, had the spirit of an angel. We loved each other." His expression darkened. "I should have known. I should have known Olivia would never have left me. I was so numbed by her betrayal, I went along with everything. But if I had seen her, if I had insisted, I would have known. I would have known it wasn't Livvie."

"Maybe that's why she refused to see you," Jeffers said, another piece of the puzzle falling into place.

"Mr. Worthy, would you like me to get your wife?" I asked.

He let out a guttural laugh. "If you had told me when I was young that one day I would be married to Shelagh Bowman . . ." He shook his head. "God, she used to drive me crazy."

"Your wife's maiden name is Bowman?" I asked.

"Yeah. So?"

The name seemed familiar somehow. I racked my brain and could see Jeffers doing the same. I hit pay dirt first.

"Jeffers, the woman at the shelter," I said. "The woman who'd been friends with Marjorie Adelman. It wasn't *Cheryl* Bowman, it was—"

"Mr. Worthy," Jeffers said, "we need to talk to your wife."

Chapter 28

"Shelagh," Duck Worthy called, running into the house with Jeffers and I close behind.

"What is it?" she asked, emerging from the kitchen and wiping her hands on a dish towel.

"These people need to talk to you."

"My heavens!" Shelagh rushed to her husband. "What on earth happened to you?"

Duck's eyes were red and most of the color had drained from his cheeks. "Never you mind. Just listen to what these folks have to say."

"Why, Detective. Ms. James. Is everything all right?"

"Mrs. Worthy, we'd like to ask you a few questions," Jeffers said.

"Of course."

Mustering up her usual cheery hospitality, Shelagh insisted on some newly baked scones and a fresh brewed pot of tea and scampered toward the kitchen.

"Leave the tea, Shelagh." Duck's voice was low and direct.

"Now, Duck, I don't see any reason to be rude. I'll only be a minute."

"Mrs. Worthy," Jeffers said, laying on the charm, "I'm afraid we really don't have time. If you'll take a seat, this should only take a few moments."

Still holding the tea towel, Shelagh settled herself into a pale yellow armchair and absent-mindedly began to fold and unfold the cloth. Duck motioned for Jeffers and me to take a seat on a floral sofa while he stood behind his wife and rested his hands gently on her shoulders.

Jeffers said, "Mrs. Worthy, do you or did you at one time know a woman by the name of Marjorie Adelman?"

"I'm afraid that name doesn't ring a bell," Shelagh twittered.

"Are you familiar with Mercy Lodge? It's a women's shelter in Niagara Falls."

Shelagh looked up to her husband.

"This is important," he said.

"I spent some time there when I was younger."

"In what capacity?" Jeffers asked.

Again she looked to her husband who gave her a reassuring nod and her shoulders a comforting squeeze. "Initially, I was there as a client," she said.

"I see," Jeffers said.

We had rightly assumed that Shelagh might have been a victim of some form of abuse, but figured it had started *after* she had married Duck. To hear that she'd been a client came as a surprise.

"You said 'initially'?" I asked, jumping in.

"My first husband was a violent man. After my rehabilitation, I chose to stay on as a volunteer. The work the shelter did back then was inspirational. I felt it was my lot to use my own experience to help other women who had gone through similar . . . ordeals."

"That's amazing," I said and Shelagh smiled at the compliment.

"Can you tell us when you worked at Mercy Lodge?" Jeffers asked.

"Oh, goodness, must have been . . . well over thirty years ago now."

"Are you sure you've never crossed paths with a Marjorie Adelman?"

We waited while Shelagh searched her memory. Finally she said, "Do you mean Joy?"

"Yes!" I said, a little too eagerly, calling to mind Lance Adelman's nickname for his wife.

"Well, yes," Shelagh said. "She came to the shelter while I was finishing up my last few months as a volunteer."

"And did you form any kind of relationship with Ms. Adelman?" Jeffers asked.

"No more so than I formed with any of the other ladies, but, yes, we spent some time together."

I flashed back to the meeting in the coffee shop with our anonymous Mercy Lodge informant and seemed to remember her telling us that Ms. Bowman had spent very little time with anyone *other* than Marjorie Adelman.

Jeffers said, "What can you remember about Marjorie . . . uh, Joy?"

"Gosh, I remember her being terrified. Her husband had been extremely violent. When she came to us her face was a horrible shade of purple. For a long while she wouldn't talk to anyone, but eventually she started to open up." Shelagh furrowed her brow. "I remember Joy's husband coming to the shelter, wanting to apologize. I certainly never believed that to be his true intention and I certainly never let him see her."

"Mrs. Worthy," Jeffers said, "did you ever talk to Joy about Olivia?"

"What?" Shelagh looked with confused eyes, first to us then to Duck.

"I need you to think carefully," Duck said.

"What's this all about?"

"I promise to explain everything," Jeffers said, "but first, in your conversations with Joy, do you recall mentioning Olivia?"

"You're starting to worry me."

"Mrs. Worthy, please. Did Olivia ever come up in conversation between you and Marjorie Adelman?"

"Of course she did. I mean, Olivia is my best friend and at that time her life was perfect. I used her as an example of the kind of life, the kind of marriage, Joy could aspire to. I wanted her to see that good things happen. That good *men* happen." Shelagh said the last sentence while looking warmly at Duck and covering one of his hands with one of hers.

"Speaking from experience," she continued, "it's so easy to lose yourself in all the pain and, when you do that, a way out seems impossible. Olivia was my bright light when *I* had needed one, and I thought maybe her story would help motivate Joy not to give up."

Shelagh stopped as her breath caught in her throat. I could see the rise and fall of her chest quicken and her hand tighten around her husband's. "Would you please tell me what this is about?" she begged. "And what any of this has to do with Olivia!"

"Would you say that your efforts were successful?" Jeffers asked. "Was Ms. Adelman inspired by Olivia's story?"

"I . . . I don't know." Shelagh was becoming more and more exasperated.

"Did she ever have anyone else visit her? Anyone besides her husband?"

"Not that I'm aware."

"Did Marjorie ever talk of another man? Someone who might have—"

"Please!" Shelagh cried through teary eyes.

"I think that's enough," Duck said.

For a few moments no one spoke. Shelagh sat with wild eyes. Duck looked like a building on the verge of collapse. Jeffers ran a hand through his hair, frustrated. There was still so much we didn't know about Marjorie's disappearance from Mercy Lodge. Who her accomplice might have been. The nature of Shelagh's relationship with Erna Weins. I doubted Shelagh would be able to provide any further information once she learned the truth about Olivia and Marjorie Adelman.

Jeffers lowered his chin into his hand. "Mrs. Worthy," he said, "what I'm about to tell you will be difficult for you to understand. I know you're going to have questions, but I need you to listen very carefully and let me finish. All right?"

Shelagh nodded.

Jeffers took a deep breath, then launched into the grisly truth.

CHAPTER 29

"I'm not sure that's what Inspector Morris meant when he said not to turn any lives upside down," I said to Jeffers when we pulled out of the driveway.

"What was I supposed to do?"

He was exhausted. Shelagh had gone from incredulous to hysterical to irate and back to hysterical. When we left, Duck was in the process of convincing his wife to take a sedative. In the course of a couple of hours we had seen Duck crumble and Shelagh fall to pieces. It didn't seem fair that we could simply walk away and leave them with the mess of their combined destruction.

"Do you think they'll call?" I asked.

After some gentle pressing by Jeffers, Duck had promised to get in touch within a couple of days when he and Shelagh had had a chance to process everything we had told them.

Jeffers shrugged.

"Look," I said, "I know you're disappointed—"

"Disappointed? Really?"

"Jeffers, I know—"

"No, you don't know!"

I decided not to push him further. The little boy needed time to pout and sulk because in his mind, he had lost the game. What he failed to acknowledge was that, in spite of the outcome, he had made great strides. I knew he'd come to understand this, but it would have to be on his own terms. Trying to force the issue would only make him withdraw further. So I sat and waited, looking out the window at the passing scenery.

After about twenty minutes Jeffers broke the silence. "I really thought Duck did it, that he and Marjorie were in on it together."

"I know. As much as I didn't want it to be true, I thought the same."

"I thought we'd come here, get him to confess, and this whole case would be solved and I could go to Morris and—"

"Jeffers, we're going to figure this out."

"Are we? Because as far as I can see, we just lost the closest thing we had to a lead."

"Okay. Yes. You're right. Duck Worthy is not Marjorie's accomplice. But, Jeffers, we—"

"*I*, Bella. *I'm* the one who has to go to Morris and tell him that *I*—"

"Stop the car!"

"We're on the highway."

"Jeffers!"

Grousing under his breath, he reluctantly brought the car to a stop on the shoulder.

"Listen to me," I said when Jeffers had turned off the ignition. "I know what this case means to you. I know what's at stake. But this isn't just about you, okay? So we didn't get the confession we were hoping for. That doesn't mean it's over. God, Jeffers, don't you see? Before today we had nothing to tie Marjorie Adelman to Olivia but now we do!"

"I don't see what that has to do—"

"It's progress! It's a piece of the puzzle we've been missing. Is it the piece that's going to complete the whole picture? No. But it's more than we had when we got in the car this morning! Look, in a couple of days, when Shelagh has had a chance to calm down and take this all in, we'll be able to get her to remember more about her time with Marjorie. Once Shelagh is a little more composed, she's going to want to share all the details she can in order to find justice for Olivia. She's the key. We just need to give her some time."

Jeffers nodded. I could sense he still wasn't fully committed to moving out from under his dark cloud, but I knew his disinclination was a child of his pigheadedness rather than a challenge to my reasoning.

"What about Erna Weins?" he asked, slightly less pouty than before.

"What about her?"

"She's tied to Shelagh, too."

"We add that to our list of things to talk to Shelagh about. When she's ready," I said, emphasizing the latter.

Jeffers knew I was right about having to wait for Shelagh but that didn't mean he had to like it. If we pushed her too soon we could risk her shutting down for good and that was simply a risk we could not afford to take.

"We don't have to wait for *Shelagh* to find out about her relationship with Erna," I said. "We could try talking to Erna again."

Jeffers chuckled. "If she 'couldn't remember' her conversation with you yesterday, what makes you think she'll be forthcoming about a phone call she had with Shelagh a couple of months ago?"

"It's worth a shot," I said.

"You know what else is worth a shot? Talking to Marjorie."

I let out an apprehensive sigh.

"I think it's time," Jeffers insisted.

We had an unspoken agreement that we would only go to Marjorie when we had irrefutable proof she couldn't talk her way out of. We'd been hoping such evidence would come in the form of her accomplice. Get him to confess and point the finger at her as the mastermind. However, as that avenue was impassable for the moment, it seemed we had to take a different approach.

"Can we wait until after the show opens?" I asked.

As much as I wanted this victory for Jeffers and as much as I wanted justice for Olivia, my Shaw debut in *Major Barbara* was important to me and, as selfish as it may have been, I didn't want anything to ruin that.

"When is the opening?"

"Saturday night."

"Okay. Your day off is Monday?"

"Yeah."

"We'll go then."

I nodded with some unease. I knew Marjorie's inevitable arrest would cast a pall on the Festival. For the first time the irony of the situation smacked me in the face. I had been so fixated on how all of our digging and poking and prodding would help Jeffers' career, I hadn't stopped to think about what it meant for my own.

"Are you okay, Samuel?"

"Yeah," I lied. "Monday's great."

Jeffers brought the car to life and nudged it back into the flow of traffic.

"Do you want to come?" I asked when the car was up to speed and we had traveled a few kilometers.

"Where?"

"To the opening?" I said. "I have two comps. If you and Aria are free . . . ?"

I had offered them to Natalie but it was the same night as an important showing for Zack and Natalie had promised to go along as supportive wife slash arm candy.

"Comps?"

"Complimentary tickets. We all get two for the opening and a few for the run of the show. If you can't use them, it's no big deal. I'll offer them around the company. I'm sure someone will jump at them. Actors never turn down free stuff."

Jeffers drove on with a contemplative smirk on his face.

"What's with the look?" I asked.

"I've never been to a play," he confessed.

"Well then," I said, "you're in for a treat."

He laughed. "How can I pass up the opportunity to see Bella James in all her glory?"

"I'm afraid it's not my glory people are interested in. This will be 'Olivia's' final opening at the Festival. That's all anyone's talking about."

I neglected to add that it would likely be my final opening as well.

CHAPTER 30

Among the many faces that made up the opening night audience were members of the press. I figured most of the reviewers would say something alluding to how my depiction of the title character could never surpass Olivia's definitive interpretation years before. As a result, I felt no pressure. Even the curiosity of seeing a TV star on stage had waned, much to my delight, and so I enjoyed my very first Shaw opening completely focused and unencumbered.

"Bella, you were awesome," Adam sang, running into my dressing room after the performance and throwing his arms around my neck.

"So were you," I said, returning the hug and meaning every word.

"Oh my God, I was terrible! Didn't you see me almost lose it when Jarod walked into the coat rack and got his pant cuff stuck on one of those flippy things on the bottom? I almost pissed my pants. Thank goodness you came in with my line. I don't know how he kept it together."

"That's because I am a professional," Jarod said, walking in on our laughter and moving to give me a congratulatory embrace. "Well done," he whispered into my ear.

His opening night card to me made the suggestion of a still hoped-for second date. I knew I would have to address it sooner or later.

"Knock, knock," Olivia said, sticking her head in through the door. "So this is where the party is."

Adam and Jarod embarrassed themselves by gushing, and Olivia ate up every kiss, squeeze and accolade.

They adored her. So had the audience. They'd applauded the moment she walked on stage and leapt to their feet when she came out to claim the final bow of the evening, a bow that should have been mine. I was the lead in the show, but under the circumstances it was only right she should have the honor.

Now I watched her as she engaged in a playful repartee with the boys. She was beautiful. This night was all about her and she knew it. And she loved it. I thought about the real Olivia and everything Marjorie had done to get to this place and this moment.

I felt my knees weaken.

"Bel!" Adam cried, reaching for me as I stumbled.

"I'm fine. Caught my heel in my hem." All eyes were on me. "I'm fine," I insisted.

"Okay everybody, get dressed quickly and get out there before those vultures eat all the food," Adam said.

It was well known that on many an opening night, the food for the reception is usually devoured by enthusiastic patrons before the starving actors get a chance to enjoy it.

"You don't have to tell me twice," Jarod said.

"You ladies are already gorgeous," Adam said on his way out. "Don't take too long."

I smiled and removed my wig. One look at the state of my hair told me I would be lucky to get a cube of cheese by the time I got out front. I'd assumed Olivia would follow the boys, but she stayed behind and closed the door.

"You were wonderful, darling," she said.

I felt a rush of love and pride emanating from her and I found myself thinking that this is how my mother might have looked at me, had she lived. In spite of everything I knew about the woman who stood before me, in that instant I wanted to rush into her arms.

"I have seen a lot of young actors come and go from this Festival. Some of them have even gone on to great things. But none of them have had your kind of talent."

She took my hands in hers, her touch warm and soothing, but I wanted her to let go. Tomorrow her world would come crashing down around her and I didn't want to remember her like this. I wanted to see her as Marjorie Adelman. It would be easier that way. Easier to accept the loss and move on.

"Bella," she said, this time taking my face in her hands, "you are the kind of actress I always wanted to be."

For a moment I was too stunned to speak. This was the closest she had ever come to alluding to her true self.

I removed her hands from my face and held them in my own. I didn't want her praise. I couldn't bear it. "You were brilliant!" I said. "Look at the audience tonight. The reaction you got when—"

She waved off my words and moved to sit on one of the two chairs in the room. "It's the abandon that you have when you're acting. The freedom. The fearlessness. Yes, I bring life to a script better than a lot of people but it's *work* for me. It's *in* you. It's effortless."

"You should have seen some of the battles I've had with my scripts," I said, taking the other chair. "I can assure you, there's been plenty of effort."

"That's the passion! That's your unbridled ability wresting for perfection! Of course you don't see it because it's a part of who you are. We always see in other people what we're lacking in ourselves. We can recognize those things instantly because they're so foreign to us. They stand out. *You* stand out."

It was true Marjorie Adelman did not have the natural talent Olivia Childries had had, but, as Peter Wynn said, she worked hard and had been rewarded with the reputation of being one of the finest actresses the country had ever known. Long before I knew the truth, I had admired the woman who sat in front of me and it would be dishonest of me to admit that her words didn't have a profound effect.

"Goodness," she said rising from her seat, "look at the time. Get out there and see for yourself. You'll see the impression you made. And do hurry," she added when she got to the door. "Adam was right about the food."

The lobby of the theatre buzzed with conversation. I had chosen to wear a sleeveless, vintage black crepe dress. Its gathered hemline fell just below my knees. My three-and-a-half-inch heels accentuated my strong calf muscles and made it look like I had the legs of a super model. I was always amazed at the magic a good pair of stilettos could weave.

I had made it halfway across the room before I received my first "congratulations" from one of the board members. The people around him followed suit and before I knew it a rippling went through the lobby and all eyes were on me. A smattering of applause started up from somewhere and made its way around the room like a wave. I managed a smile and nodded my thanks at the warm reception. I caught the eye of our director in the distance. She gave me a wink before resuming her conversation. Suddenly the applause went from modest to thundering.

I turned to see Olivia looking radiant in a violet, one-shoulder dress. She accepted the ovation with much more grace than I had, and immediately began to receive her throng of well-wishers with a warmth that would have led anyone to believe that each and every person in the room was one of her closest acquaintances.

Peter Wynn appeared at her side with a glass of champagne.

He ushered his starlet from one set of adoring fans to the next as if he was responsible for her glory. It occurred to me that in some way, he actually was. He caught my eye and the two of us stood staring at one another for a passing moment. Contrary to the arrogance of his outward show, I could see the pain in the windows of his eyes and I turned away.

Though I was relieved to have the attention off of me, I felt a fleeting disappointment at how quickly the favor had turned.

I felt a hand on my back and found myself being led through the open doors and out into the courtyard, where it was far less occupied and much easier to breathe. I turned to thank my savior and found myself looking into a sea of perfect green.

"You looked like you needed rescuing," said Dr. Gorgeous.

"Yeah, thanks," I said, lost in the spell of his eyes.

"You look incredible," he said, and quickly followed it up with, "I got you this." He handed me a paper plate of hors d'oeuvres. "Manda said there's never anything left for the actors so . . . I hope I got things you like."

I'd forgotten Manda was responsible for him being there. In spite of her involvement, I was rendered speechless by his thoughtfulness. "Thank you," I said in a tone I hoped communicated how genuinely touched I was by his gesture.

He seemed to read me perfectly and grinned adorably, obviously pleased that I was pleased. "The show was amazing," he said. "You were unbelievable. I can't remember when I've been so emotionally invested in a production."

"Oh, thank you! Of course Olivia was spectacular. She really brought a life and energy to this piece that we all fed off of. She—"

"It wasn't just Olivia."

I smiled and lowered my eyes as I felt the color rising in my cheeks. I'd never been able to take compliments well. "Well," I said, changing the subject, "the least I could do, after you braved life and limb getting me a plate of food, is share." I gestured toward an open table next to the rectangular pool that served as the courtyard's centerpiece.

"I'm always amazed at how you actors remember all those lines," he said, reaching for a carrot stick and dipping it in hummus.

I stifled the urge to roll my eyes. Non-actors always think the memorization is the hardest part about acting when, in fact, it's one of the easiest. Their astonishment at what they seem to think is a super power is always one of the first things people comment on, and is one of the last things any actor wants to hear.

Dr. Gorgeous, for his part, could be entirely forgiven simply because he had assumed correctly that all that memorization can make an actress hungry.

"It's really no different than you having to memorize all the procedures you have to do, or being able to diagnose a patient by looking at symptoms. Somewhere in your brain, you have all that information filed away, otherwise you'd have to check a book every ten seconds."

"Hmm," he said, "I've never thought about it that way. I guess you're not that remarkable after all or maybe *I* deserve much more credit around the office." He winked and we both laughed as much as our full mouths would allow.

"There you are." Manda's voice rang out from the threshold of the glass door that separated the lobby from the outdoors. "I've been looking everywhere for you. I thought I told you I'd meet you by the bar." Manda held two glasses of wine.

"Sorry," Dr. Gorgeous said. "I wanted to make sure Bella got something to eat before everything was picked over."

The expression on Manda's face showed that she did not appreciate his gesture as much as I did. "Good show, Bel," she said flatly, acknowledging my presence briefly before turning her attention back to her date. "Come on," she urged, "there's someone I want you to meet."

"It was lovely to see you," he said to me.

I nodded and watched him go.

"Who's Mr. Dark and Handsome?" Jeffers said, coming through the doorway.

"Hush."

Jeffers and Aria came bearing wine and big congratulatory hugs.

"I see you survived your first trip to the theatre," I teased.

"I did," Jeffers replied. "I'm not sure I'd choose it again over a hockey game but—"

"Oh, for goodness sake, it's important to try new things," Aria said. "I've been trying to get him to the theatre for years. Bella, you were fantastic! And, oh my God, your dress! You look stunning."

"Yeah, Samuel, you clean up good," Jeffers said, helping himself to a mini-quiche.

"I can't wait to fit into my dresses again," Aria said. "I feel like a blimp."

"Are you kidding me?" I said. "You could probably fit into this dress, baby bump and all!"

"So who was that guy you were cozying up to?" Jeffers asked again.

"He's nobody and we're not talking about it."

"Sure didn't look like nobody," Jeffers persisted with a twinkle in his eye.

"He's Moustache's vet," I said.

"And?"

"And we're not talking about it."

"Andre, leave her alone," Aria said. "He was pretty cute though," she added with a giggle and excused herself to go to the bathroom.

"So, the show's open. Now what?" Jeffers asked.

"Now we run for the next few months. We don't have any more rehearsals, though. Not for this show anyway. I start rehearsals for the other show in two weeks."

"What's that one about?"

"It's Harold Pinter," I said. "You won't like it."

"I was kidding about the hockey. Tell me."

"It's called *The Hothouse*. It's about a murder and rape that take place in a corrupt institution."

"That sounds like more my style."

"Don't you get enough of that at work?"

Jeffers nodded. "Speaking of which, you all set for Monday?"

I pushed my plate off to the side. "What time?"

"I can go alone."

I shook my head. I had gotten too deeply involved, and was determined to see it through to the end. A laugh erupted inside the theatre. Jeffers and I both turned to look. Olivia was holding court in the middle of a group of people who were hanging on her every word.

"Look at her," I said to Jeffers. "Isn't she beautiful? She dazzles everybody she comes into contact with. It doesn't matter who she is underneath. Tonight she's Olivia Childries and she's magnificent." I felt tears brim.

Jeffers rose and put a hand on my shoulder. "I'll call you Monday morning," he said, quietly, leaving me feeling like Judas at the Last Supper.

CHAPTER 31

I arrived home after one. The party had still been going strong when I left and I had managed to sneak out with little fanfare. Standing on my porch, I looked across the street to where Erna Weins lived. Her house was dark, which wasn't unusual for this time of night. What was unusual was that it had been dark for days.

Jeffers had gone by every day to talk to Erna about Shelagh Worthy. At one point I wondered aloud if Erna might be dead, which prompted him to walk the perimeter of her property, peering in windows, checking for any signs of foul play. During his last visit, a neighbor told him Erna had asked her to feed her cats while she went out of town. After a little digging of my own, I learned she'd gone to visit a daughter in Oshawa. Until she returned, Erna and Shelagh's association would remain a mystery.

Letting myself into my cottage, I was overwhelmed by the aroma of flowers. Natalie and Zack had sent a lovely bouquet, as did my agent. Although Dean had encouraged me to distance myself from film and TV for a while, most of his money was made in that medium. When my opening night coincided with the screening of another one of his client's movies, he walked the red carpet and I got flowers. In addition, I'd been given a stunning spray of freesias from Olivia, a trio of roses from Jarod, and some potted tulips from the director.

I was trimming the roses when Moustache finally came to

greet me. He walked sleepily into the kitchen, yawned while in his downward dog, and did a little dance by the back door. I let him out.

Despite the late hour and the long week that had preceded it, I was wide awake. I poured myself half a glass of wine, hoping it would make me drowsy and slow my racing thoughts of Olivia.

I looked at her beautiful flowers and the card that accompanied them and thought about the wonderful things she had said to me in the dressing room. I marveled that this could be the same woman who had committed murder and fraud.

Emptying the glass of wine, I let Moustache in and we raced up the stairs to begin our nightly routine, which involved me breaking a Milk Bone into three pieces and hiding them within the folds of the blankets on the bed. With his heightened sense of smell, finding the treats should have been easy, but never a night went by that I didn't have to give him some kind of subtle clue. He then chewed his found treasure, full of pride over his accomplishment, unaware of my intervention.

Moustache circled on top of my pillows before plopping himself down and flopping over onto his back. I knew he would eventually jump down to his own cushion, so I took full advantage of the snuggle time and drifted off to sleep with my hand on his belly.

After having passed a rather dull Sunday, I awoke Monday to the sound of birds. The sun was glorious, streaming through my window, bathing the room in gold. The sky was a bright blue. A perfect day for a lynching.

Jeffers arrived just before ten thirty. In the kitchen, over tea and croissants, we laid out our plan.

"I don't think we should mention Marjorie Adelman right off the bat. She might lawyer up and then we'll never get answers," I said.

"I disagree," Jeffers said. "She's a master manipulator. For all intents and purposes she's been Olivia Childries longer than Olivia Childries was. If we start asking questions, she's going to dance around the subject for as long as she can, trying to ascertain how much we actually know. She'll flip the tables on us. And when she gets all the information she needs, she'll ask us to leave without admitting to anything. Might even threaten us with harassment, and that will be the last we see of her. I say we go in and drop the bomb right away. Catch her off guard. If she lawyers up, that's an admission of guilt as far as I'm concerned. Whether she answers my questions or tells the story in front of a jury, the truth is bound to come out. My job today is to make an arrest and get this case one step closer to solved."

"Hmm," I said.

"You don't agree?"

"I don't know," I said on the snappish side of defensive. "I've only ever done this on TV."

"I know she's your friend," Jeffers said.

"I'm an actress," I said. "I live things like this all the time on screen. Or in a play. But after the scene's been shot or the show is over, I'm done. I get to go home. But this is real! These are people's lives! What we did to the Worthys . . . what we're about to do to Olivia . . ."

I stopped talking before I brought up what this case meant for my career. I had promised myself I wouldn't lay that on Jeffers and had every intention of keeping my word. I shook the thought out of my head and said, "It's easier for you."

"I'm sorry. I should have been more sensitive. I keep forgetting you're a civilian. For the record, Bella, it's never easy."

Olivia answered the door. She wore a soft pink, silk Charmeuse tie-neck blouse and a pair of white capris. She smiled when she saw us.

"Bella, I was just about to call you! Did you see the reviews?"

I shook my head.

"They are wonderful!" she said, beaming. "You, my darling, are a star! One of the papers said—"

"Olivia, I'm afraid this isn't a social call."

Her eyes narrowed. She looked to me and then to Jeffers, maintaining her smile.

"We have a few questions," Jeffers said, "for Marjorie Adelman."

Olivia's smile faltered.

"Well then," she said, "you'd better come in."

CHAPTER 32

"I started having the memories several years ago," Olivia said. "They weren't anything I could explain, not definitively. They were by no means extraordinary. Just flashes of another life. I couldn't even say for certain if it was my life."

"Can you give us some examples?" Jeffers asked.

"I'd be somewhere and I'd have a flash of having been there before or someplace like it. Or I'd see someone and all of a sudden there would be this image in my head of a person bearing a very strong resemblance. But I never could identify who it was."

"Did you ever mention these flashes to anyone? Your doctor? A friend?"

"At first, no. Following my . . . accident . . . the doctors diagnosed me with traumatic amnesia."

"Is that the kind where victims of traumatic events block out certain memories because they're too hard to process?" I asked.

"Not quite," she said. "Traumatic amnesia is a direct result of brain damage. The duration of the amnesia is related to the extent of the injury. In my case, I suffered severe damage to the limbic system of my brain. The doctors informed me there was a possibility I would never recover *any* memories of my past."

"Do you remember being Marjorie Adelman?" Jeffers said.

Olivia sighed. "No."

"But when we mentioned that name at the front door, you seemed to—"

"How can I explain?" Olivia asked no one in particular.

I could see Jeffers was frustrated. We had both been caught off guard by the calm with which Olivia had invited us into her home. Almost like she had been expecting us. Not *us*, exactly, but somebody demanding answers. What was odd, however, was that nothing in her behavior gave any indication of guilt. Or of remorse. Either she was more cold-blooded than I thought, or there was a lot more to the story than Jeffers and I had anticipated.

"Ms. Adelman," Jeffers started.

"Olivia," she said with pleading eyes. "Please. I may have been Marjorie Adelman once, but my life as Olivia Childries is the only one I've known, so . . . please."

Jeffers nodded. "Olivia," he said, "you mentioned you didn't tell anyone about your memories 'at first.' Can I take this to mean you did tell someone?"

"The doctors had said there was a *possibility* that my memories would never return which, to me, meant there was also a possibility they would. *Possibility* gave me something to hope for, you see." She paused and vanished inside herself for a moment. "The elation I felt when the flashes began . . . you see, I had never stopped believing. I knew the flashes were my memories fighting through the amnesia. I didn't say anything right away. I held on to the hope that the day would come when my past would flood over me. I would feel whole again. Feel like myself. I scoured the photo albums Shelagh made for me, looking for one of the faces I had seen in my head. Looking for *anything* that would corroborate the memories."

"What happened?" I asked

"There was no flood. The flashes never became more than just that. Not really surprising, is it? The memories in those albums weren't mine to begin with, were they? Ultimately, I got tired of waiting for it to happen, so I went to my psychiatrist, hoping there was some medical thing that could hurry it along.

There wasn't. Shelagh was wonderful when I told her. She would have me describe in the greatest possible detail everything I could remember whenever I had one of the little déjà vu feelings. She would try to fit them into her own library of recollections in the hope they would trigger something but over time I got more and more depressed and, in the end, my doctor prescribed some antidepressants."

I shot Jeffers a look. The pills he had stolen during Olivia's Easter celebration had been labeled as antidepressants but were nothing of the kind.

"What happened when you started taking the medication?" Jeffers asked.

"The memories stopped," Olivia said.

"They stopped?"

Olivia nodded. "I had one or two at the beginning of the prescription, but then they stopped altogether."

"And what's the name of your doctor?"

"Dr. David Lin."

"And you're still taking antidepressants?"

"Detective," Olivia said, "I'm sure you can imagine how difficult it is to feel normal when there is a part of you that can never be reached locked inside your brain. To be perfectly honest, I was relieved when the flashes stopped. I was no longer being teased by something I could never have."

Although incredibly convenient, I felt the amnesia story was genuine.

"I still don't understand how you knew about Marjorie Adelman," I said.

"That was fate, pure and simple."

She rose and disappeared into the living room. When she returned, she held a yellowing piece of newspaper.

"About two years ago I came across an article in the paper about a woman who had been killed in a house fire. There was something about her picture that . . . spoke to me. She seemed familiar somehow. I couldn't explain it. I had never met her. Her name meant nothing to me. There was just something about her picture."

She unfolded the paper and took a moment to look fondly at the image before handing it over to Jeffers. There was a picture of the charred remains of a townhouse along with photographs of the fire's two victims, a man, Abe Daniels, and his wife, Violet.

"Marjorie's sister," Jeffers and I said together, recalling our visit with Lance Adelman.

Olivia nodded. "I was so taken by this photograph that I went to the visitation."

I glanced back at the article and saw the details for the viewing and funeral arrangements were included in its conclusion.

"I hadn't thought about what I was going to do when I got there. I was just guided by impulse. When I arrived, the funeral home was almost at capacity. It was easy to slip in unnoticed. I didn't recognize a soul. Not that I had really expected to. No one recognized me, either. I was drawn to a memorial someone had put together. Pictures of the two people who had been killed."

Olivia was speaking as if in a trance. Like she was reliving the moment.

"There was one photograph of Violet standing with her arm around another woman," she continued. "They couldn't have been more than twenty. They were both making funny faces at the camera. I recognized the other woman instantly. I knew as soon as I looked into her eyes that I was looking at myself."

She paused a moment before continuing. "I asked around and learned the woman with Violet in that picture was her sister Marjorie. Answers to some of my other questions told me that her married name was Adelman and that she hadn't been heard from in many years. Most people assumed she'd died. Her disappearance was a loss Violet had never fully recovered from. For months I tried to find out anything I could about Marjorie Adelman."

"Did you ever have any tests done?" Jeffers asked. "DNA?"

"I didn't have to. I *knew*. It was the first time since the accident that I had ever been so comfortable in my own skin."

"But just to be certain?"

"There was an old woman at the funeral home. Violet's aunt. She sat in her wheelchair, off to the side, observing the crowd. When her eyes caught mine she called out to me."

"Marjorie?" I asked.

Olivia nodded. "One of her attendants went to comfort her and I could hear her assuring the old woman there was no possible way Marjorie could be there. No one realized it was me she had been calling to. I'm sure they passed it off as senility. So you see, I don't need any tests. I know I'm Marjorie Adelman. And I know Olivia Childries is dead. And I can only assume by your being here that I had something to do with that. Am I right?"

Chapter 33

Jeffers showed Olivia the mug shot of Marjorie Adelman and filled her in on the details of her tumultuous relationship with Lance. Olivia soaked up every detail without interrupting. When Jeffers finished, she rose and stood with her back to us, gazing out the floor to ceiling windows that separated us from the gorgeous day outside.

"So I met Shelagh at the shelter?"

"Yes," Jeffers said. "She was a volunteer there and the two of you became quite close."

"Shelagh told us," I said carefully, "that she remembered telling you, um, Marjorie about her friend Olivia, hoping you would see that a perfect life was possible. To give you something to aspire to. To live for."

"You spoke with Shelagh?"

"We interviewed her as part of this investigation," Jeffers said.

"So she knows I'm—"

"It was necessary to inform her so, yes. We believe—"

"I think it's very clear what you believe. You think I killed Olivia and took her place in order to escape the hell I was living in. Am I close?"

Our combined silence provided Olivia with the answer.

"And did I beat myself up, too?" she asked, turning to face us. "Don't answer that. I know where this is going."

"How did you know Olivia was dead?" Jeffers asked.

"I'm sorry?"

"You said you knew Olivia was dead. I'm curious as to how."

She let out a long sigh. "A couple of months ago I got a call from Shelagh asking me to drop off a check to a woman named Erna Weins. It was a donation of some kind. A charity. I can't remember which. I was surprised. Shelagh's husband had come across some records of her charitable transactions and had been astounded at the amount. I was, too, when she told me. But that's Shelagh. Always a bleeding heart for a good cause. Anyway, she had promised Duck she would cut back but, for whatever reason, this particular charity had touched her dear heart and she said she wouldn't be able to live with herself if she didn't do something to help. She promised to pay me back. That way her trail was covered, as far as Duck was concerned. I didn't care about the money and I knew it meant a great deal to Shelagh, so I said I'd do it."

"What happened when you got there?" I asked, already knowing that the meeting had ended with Olivia peeling out of Erna Weins' driveway at breakneck speed.

"The whole thing was very strange. When I introduced myself she said how nice it was to see me again. I figured we must have met at some Shaw function and dismissed it. When I explained I was dropping off a donation on Shelagh's behalf, her mood changed. She took the check but didn't seem overly appreciative, in my opinion. Five thousand dollars is a very generous donation."

"Five thousand dollars!" I exclaimed.

Olivia smiled. "Shelagh doesn't do anything small. And besides, she can afford it. She comes from money. A lot of it. And there's no chance of it running out in her lifetime, believe me. At least she's using it for good."

"Then why was her husband so concerned?"

"From what I gather, Duck is a self-made man. Worked for every cent he has. He and Shelagh see money very differently."

"From what you gather?" I asked.

"I've never met the man. Never even spoke to him."

"But you were married to him!"

"Ah," she corrected, "but I wasn't, was I?"

"Of course. I'm sorry."

"Getting back to your meeting with Mrs. Weins," Jeffers said. "You gave her the check. Then what?"

"Then she said something that made my blood turn cold. She said, 'Awful thing about those bones being discovered at your old house.' With that one sentence, I knew the bones were Olivia's and that somehow her death had facilitated my being. I'm afraid I was very rude to Mrs. Weins. I left her so quickly."

"Hadn't you ever wondered what had happened to the real Olivia?" Jeffers asked. "After you made the discovery about Marjorie?"

"Of course I wondered," Olivia said, her voice rising. "But I never dreamed I could have . . . I convinced myself there *had* to be another explanation. Even with you sitting here today, I cannot believe I could have been desperate enough to . . ." A single tear rolled down her cheek. She couldn't even bring herself to say the words. "Are you going to arrest me?"

CHAPTER 34

I could barely keep up to Jeffers as we left Olivia's house.

"Jeffers?" I panted when I reached the car and let myself in to its passenger side.

He held up a finger to silence me and pulled out his phone. "This is Detective Sergeant Jeffers," he said. "I need the address of a Dr. David Lin."

After a moment, he punched an address into his GPS.

"You got time for another stop?" he asked, buckling his seatbelt.

"Do you want to tell me what this is about?"

"Olivia's antidepressants."

"What about them? You told me the pill you stole was a placebo laced with something."

"Lopressor, a beta-blocker that's prescribed to patients with heart disease. At the time, we assumed Marjorie Adelman was using it to administer to a part of her past."

"But there was nothing in Marjorie's file to indicate—"

"I don't know why I didn't think of it before. For a few years now there's been research that shows beta-blockers can also impede the brain's ability to make and remake memories. Every time a person recalls a memory that elicits a particularly emotional or stressful response, the brain recreates the memory so the person essentially relives the experience. What beta-blockers do is inhibit the brain from renewing the memory."

"So, the memory is erased?"

"Not erased, exactly, but suppressed. As long as the beta-blocker is in the system, the person is protected from accessing whatever painful memories might exist."

"Are you telling me you think someone is deliberately trying to make sure Olivia doesn't remember her life as Marjorie?"

"Olivia said that soon after she started taking the anti-depressants, her flashes stopped."

"Flashes that caused Olivia a great amount of emotional stress. Oh my God, Jeffers, her doctor could be involved!"

"And if he's not, maybe he can tell us who is."

Dr. Lin's receptionist was none too pleased about our unscheduled appointment.

"He's in the middle of a session and has a very full calendar," she said.

Jeffers threatened to arrest her for impeding an investigation, and she begrudgingly picked up the phone to inform the doctor of our presence.

"The police are here to see you," she grumbled into the receiver. Then she hung up the phone and said, "Have a seat. He'll be with you in a few minutes."

As we turned toward the waiting area, we heard hard-soled shoes hurrying along the tiled corridor.

"Officers," a man's voice called out, his hand outstretched and his smile warm. "I'm David Lin." He shook each of our hands in turn. "Is there something I can help you with?"

"I'm Detective Sergeant Jeffers and this is my partner and we shouldn't need more than a few minutes. I understand you're a very busy man." Jeffers subtly directed this last statement toward the reception desk.

Dr. Lin led Jeffers and me into his office. While he took the chair behind his desk, Jeffers and I entered into a silent negotiation over who would take over the only other remaining chair in the office and who would occupy the proverbial couch. I made a beeline for the chair.

Dr. Lin was a tall man of distant Chinese heritage. Looking at the dates of the various degrees and certificates adorning the walls, I estimated his age to be early to middle fifties. Some quick mental math told me there was no possible way Dr. Lin could have been the psychiatrist who treated Olivia immediately following the accident, leaving me to wonder how long the two of them had known each other and, also, how well.

"Doctor, I understand one of your patients is Olivia Chil-dries," Jeffers said. "I know you are bound by confidentiality and I have every intention of respecting that. However, I'm hoping those confines allow for the answers to a few questions."

"Thank you," Dr. Lin said, "and if it makes your job easier, I'm happy to extend that courtesy to you and your partner as well."

"Thank you, it would."

With Dr. Lin's assurance of discretion, Jeffers launched into Olivia's story, presenting enough of the details the doctor would need to be of help to us. He listened intently until Jeffers finished, then punched a button on his intercom and told his receptionist to cancel the rest of his appointments. Then he reclined in his chair and closed his eyes.

"Let's start with Olivia's prescription," he said, moving to a file cabinet behind his desk and retrieving Olivia's file. "I prescribed Celexa Oral about three years ago. As she told you, she believed she was finally beginning to have memories of her past and was growing increasingly frustrated because they never lasted for more than a few instants. She was desperate for them to last longer and begin to mean something. We talked at length about the extent of her injuries and the possibility that her flashes would never become more than just that and, I'm sure you can imagine, she became more dejected. With each visit I could see her withdrawing deeper into a depression. It was starting to affect her work and her relationships. The pills were prescribed to provide her with some relief so she could go about her life."

"Would the Celexa Oral have any effect on her memory flashes?"

Dr. Lin shook his head. "Antidepressants help with mood. Of course, when altering the chemicals of the brain, there are side effects, but any sort of play on memory function is highly unlikely."

"Doctor, are you familiar with the research that has been conducted on Lopressor and other similar beta-blockers with regard to their memory eradicating abilities?"

Dr. Lin gave a small chuckle. "Do you remember the movie *Eternal Sunshine of a Spotless Mind?* Two people meet by supposed chance only to learn that they were former lovers who each had their memories of the other person erased."

Both Jeffers and I nodded.

"After that movie came out, I was inundated with clients wanting me to prescribe the same treatment, and all were disappointed to learn the procedure in the film was fictitious, entertainment. Imagine my surprise when I read an article about some Dutch researchers developing a memory-erasing pill using beta-blockers. At the time, the research was under ethical scrutiny and, to be perfectly honest, I've heard rumblings about such advancements since then but never really paid it too much mind. The quick and easy fix is not the kind of treatment I want to promote. It's not healthy. Not in the long run. For my part, even prescribing antidepressants has to come out of exhaustive efforts to solve the issue without the aid of any medication. There are doctors who are little more than drug dispensers. I am not one of them."

"How easy would it be for someone to find out about a drug

with this capability?"

"Detective, you know as well as I do the internet can be a wonderful thing in many ways. And if the internet isn't your thing, there are plenty of people on the street who would be happy to hook you up . . . for the right price."

"In your opinion, do you think Olivia would have been desperate enough to resort to such measures?"

"In my opinion? No. She was desperate to learn about her past. That desperation made her ill. If she was going to turn to any kind of drug, it would have been one that possessed the possibility of extracting memories, not erasing them."

"Doctor, where do your patients get their prescriptions filled?"

"There's a pharmacy on the first floor. Many of them go there out of convenience."

"And the pharmacist?"

"Are you asking if I think he would tamper with the prescription?"

"Someone had to. And he wouldn't be the first pharmacist to be guilty of such a thing."

"Mr. Avery has been the pharmacist here since before I took over the practice. I can't believe he could possibly be responsible for something like that."

"You can't believe, but you don't know for certain, right? People can be tempted by the smallest things."

"How long have you been treating Olivia?" I said, changing the subject.

"Almost twenty years. I was very young to have her under my care, but I took over my father's practice as soon as I finished my training. She had been a patient of his for some time. Trusted him completely. I'm sure that's why she chose to stay when my father stepped down."

"So it was your father who would have treated Olivia immediately following her attack?"

"That's correct."

"In her conversations with him," Jeffers said, "did she ever indicate—"

"I have to stop you there, Detective. I've already disclosed information that I shouldn't have, by law. I did it because it was information that she, herself, has shared with you. I cannot disclose anything else that was said in any of her sessions with myself or my father before me."

"Of course."

I said, "Did Olivia ever undergo any hypnosis to help with her amnesia?"

After a beat, Dr. Lin admitted she had. "Shortly after the flashes started," he said. "She thought it might help."

"And under hypnosis, was she able to remember anything from the night of the attack?"

Dr. Lin hesitated then said, "She was not able to remember any details about the attack itself."

"What about before the attack?" Jeffers asked.

"I'm sorry." Dr. Lin shook his head.

"Doctor," I said, "forgive me, but you didn't seem all that surprised when we mentioned Marjorie Adelman."

"Again, because Ms. Childries was candid with you on this matter, I can tell you she was very open about her feelings of detachment from her life as Olivia. She always felt she was intruding on another person's existence. When she discovered the photograph of Marjorie Adelman, the clouds parted and she could see clearly for the first time. Knowing the truth was a huge relief for her. However, the frustration at not being able to access any of her memories without the aid of hypnosis eventually grew too much for her and the therapy was abandoned."

"Did she tell you she thought she might have killed the real Olivia Childries?" Jeffers asked. When the doctor nodded, Jeffers said, "I don't think she did."

It was the first time since leaving Olivia's that Jeffers had shared his thoughts about her guilt. Or innocence. Our conversation during our trip to Dr. Lin's office had been centered on the drugs. Neither of us had actually voiced what we felt about Olivia's admission, or what bearing it had on the case. Ever since we had started investigating, we were of the mind that Olivia had been the one who had orchestrated the murder and subsequent identity theft. It had never occurred to me that she might, in fact, be a victim in this case.

"I think whoever is responsible for altering Olivia's medication is directly tied to her attack and the murder of the real Olivia Childries," Jeffers continued. "Someone does not want Olivia remembering her past. We still don't know the reason why but I think we're close. I have one more question and then I promise we'll go."

Dr. Lin was speechless. He wasn't the only one. He nodded.

"You said Olivia was desperate to regain her memories. Even before she knew they were Marjorie's."

"That's right."

"In your professional opinion, did you ever find it odd that someone so desperate would purposely shut out a person who was such an important part of her past? Someone who might have been the key to unlocking that door?"

"Who are you talking about?"

"Duck Worthy."

"Olivia's first husband? But Olivia didn't shut him out."

Jeffers looked like a puzzle piece had just slipped into place. I, however, was incredulous.

"She refused to see him after the attack," I said. "She never saw him through the divorce. She's best friends with his wife and she has never—"

"She tried, on many occasions, to meet with him. My father even encouraged her to invite him to one of her sessions."

I looked from the doctor to Jeffers and back to the doctor again. Jeffers took no notice of me. He was already putting pieces together while I sat amid the mess.

"What happened?" I finally asked.

"He wouldn't come," Dr. Lin said. "He refused to speak to her. He shut *her* out, not the other way around."

"Jeffers, what's going on?" I asked when we were in the elevator. "All that stuff about Olivia being innocent. And that business about Duck."

Jeffers kept hitting the button repeatedly, agitatedly, as if this action would propel the elevator to increase its speed. The entire trip involved five stops and by the time the elevator had deposited us in the building's lobby, Jeffers was like a caged animal finally freed. He darted to the front doors with me stumbling after him.

"The pharmacy's over there," I said, pointing to the sign hanging above the entrance to the store and nearly tripping in the process.

"We're not going to the pharmacy," he said, pushing open the door to the outside and heading for the car.

"But I thought—"

"Change of plans. Hurry up!"

I had learned how to do some basic stunt work on *Port Authority* and used some of this knowledge to make it look like I slammed my fingers in the car door. Jeffers popped the trunk and rummaged around for a first-aid kit, releasing his grip on the car keys as he did so. I slipped the key ring around my index finger and abruptly ceased my performance. Jeffers looked up, just as abruptly, and bumped his head on the hatch.

"We're not going anywhere until you tell me what's going on," I said, dangling the keys while he rubbed the back of his head.

205

"Olivia's not involved," Jeffers announced with absolute certainty as we settled ourselves on the front seat. "Even if she had planned the murder and hired someone to disfigure her face, and even if it was her accomplice from long ago who was feeding her tainted medication in order to cover his own ass, it doesn't make sense. Which brings us to Duck."

"What? I thought we agreed there was no way Duck could have murdered Olivia!"

"He didn't. Dr. Lin said Olivia had made repeated attempts to meet with Duck following the accident. But this morning—"

"Olivia said she'd never even spoken to him."

"And Duck said Olivia refused to have any contact with him after the attack."

"So you think someone has been deliberately keeping Olivia and Duck apart for all these years?"

"Absolutely. Because if Duck saw Olivia, he would know she wasn't really his wife."

"Because of the eyes," I said, recalling Duck's words at our last meeting.

"And who is the only person with enough influence over both of them to be able to pull off such a feat? And who would have access to Olivia in order to switch out the real pills with the laced ones?"

"Shelagh."

CHAPTER 35

Inspector Morris sat for a long while without speaking. Jeffers and I sat across from him in his office, afraid to breathe. Jeffers had laid out our evidence and relayed the details of what had led to our current theory that Shelagh Worthy was somehow involved in Olivia's murder and the plan to use Marjorie Adelman to cover it up.

It was a theory that made the most sense, but I still found it hard to wrap my head around the probability that the sweet woman who liked to flirt and make pies could be an evil mastermind. I pictured Shelagh as a cartoon super-villain, a big insignia of a rolling pin on her chest and her floral apron acting as a cape. I disguised a snicker as a cough and caught a look from Morris.

"What else do we know about this Worthy woman?" Morris asked.

"We've told you everything," Jeffers said. "Up to now, we haven't had any reason to suspect her."

"Well then, you'd better get on. You said she was a victim of spousal abuse. Perhaps she filed an official complaint. Check the archives and see where that leads you."

"Yes, sir." Jeffers rose and I followed suit.

"Before you head downstairs," Morris said, stopping our retreat, "sit down with Raines. I want him kept up to speed."

Jeffers shoulders slumped ever so slightly.

"Ms. James," Morris said, "I think Sergeant Jeffers can take it from here."

I was struck a little dumb at my sudden dismissal. My mouth finally managed a "Thank you, sir," which, once said, propelled Jeffers and me out of the room.

"So that's it? I'm done?" I asked when we were out of earshot.

"Go home and get some rest, Samuel," Jeffers said. "It's your day off. You might as well salvage what you can of it."

"Are you serious? How am I supposed to just go home and carry on like I'm not involved? See Olivia every day and pretend like I don't know her life is falling apart and how I'm partly responsible for that? We promised each other that we would see this through to the end!"

"Bella—"

"God, Jeffers, it's not just *your* career on the line here!" The last sentence came out of sheer emotion and I regretted it the minute I had put the exclamation point on it.

"What do you mean?"

"I'm not sure how my involvement in the . . . exposure . . . of Olivia Childries is going to be regarded within the industry."

"You think you'll be blackballed?"

"I don't know."

"Shit, Bella!"

Jeffers criticized and I defended my participation in the case. We attracted an audience, and he pulled me into a storage closet where our voices lowered and our tempers calmed.

"Jeffers, I have no regrets. Believe me. Neither of us knows what's going to happen when this is all over. We may both be out of work. But we've come so far. I can't be off the case."

"What are you talking about? You're not off the case."

"But Inspector Morris said—"

"Bella, Morris said I have to take it from here because my

next few hours are going to be spent in the dungeon where they keep the archives and no civilians, not even consultants, are given access to those files."

"So I'm not 'done'?"

"You're done for today," he said with a smile.

I closed my eyes and bit my lower lip, feeling every inch the fool. "I'm sorry."

"Look, I was serious about you enjoying whatever's left of your day off. Go home. Walk Moustache. Have a glass of wine and try to relax. Believe me you don't want to sit across from Raines while I fill him in. I promise to call if I find out anything."

I nodded and turned to go.

"Hey," Jeffers called after me, "I knew there was a drama queen in there somewhere."

Jeffers found a young officer who looked like he'd barely survived puberty to drive me home. He was so starstruck at meeting Emma Samuel, he tried to keep his cool, but as I regaled him with stories from the *Port Authority* set and uttered a few of Emma's classic lines and shared some behind-the-scenes secrets, he was certifiably giddy by the time we pulled up in front of my house. I watched him drive away and caught a small movement through the window that looked into Erna Weins' kitchen.

I knew it was probably her cat, but I crossed the road and knocked gently on her door.

"Erna?" I knocked again, a little louder. "Erna? It's Bella James from across the street."

I raised my hand to knock once more and jumped as the door moved inward. Erna peeked out. She looked up and down both sides of the street before meeting my eyes. "You shouldn't be here," she said.

"Erna, please. It's important. I promise you're not in any trouble."

"You have no idea," she said. "What I've done could get me in all kinds of trouble."

CHAPTER 36

"Erna, what kind of trouble? What do you mean?" I asked as she ushered me inside her house.

"They can't know I talked to you," she said, gathering her sweater around her and pursing her lips.

"Erna, who's 'they'?"

"I knew something wasn't right. But they told me they would . . . She gave me . . ."

"Erna," I said, doing my very best to squelch my growing frustration, "*who* told you?"

She shook her head, clearly terrified. I knew whatever secret she was keeping was key to this investigation. Jeffers and I had been trying to get her to talk to us for weeks and I was not going to blow this opportunity by scaring her off. I counted to three before assuming my most comforting tone.

"Erna, I promise you, they . . . Shelagh . . . won't know you talked to me about this." She didn't correct me so I went on. "As far as anyone else is concerned, my being here right now is nothing more than one neighbor asking another to borrow an egg." I smiled and took her hand in mine. "I promise you."

I didn't know what I was promising exactly. I was in no position to promise protection, nor could I promise not to divulge her secrets. However, I wholly believed she would be safe, and, luckily, Erna believed it, too. She led me into the sitting room, drew the drapes, and joined me on the sofa.

"I didn't start suspecting anything until they found those

bones." She looked regretful, like somehow she should have known better. "I've always been very curious about the goings on in the neighborhood," she said, and I smiled at her delicate way of admitting she was nosy. "It was the day that actress—Olivia—was attacked. I remember there being so many things happening at her house that day."

"Like what?"

"Well, the flowers for one thing. It seemed like one delivery after another. I noticed a change in Olivia as the day went on. She grew more and more tired. A man came by in the early evening and her husband a little after that. A big, tall man, her husband. Very nice. I couldn't believe it when Shelagh told me he had . . . he was always very nice, you see. They both were. And so much in love."

"Erna, was there anything else about that day that struck you as *especially* odd?"

"I found it strange that her husband went back out again. He always came home at the same time and was in for the night."

"How did her husband look when he left?"

"Oh, I didn't see his face. Just saw him get in the car and drive off."

"And the other man? Did you see him leave?"

"Yes. He left about fifteen minutes after her husband. He was obviously distressed about something."

I knew she was referring to Peter Wynn and I knew, from Peter's own account, what had transpired in that house. "Distressed" was an understatement.

So far Erna Weins had not told me anything I didn't already know. I needed to get her talking about Shelagh. "Erna, was Shelagh there that night?"

She swallowed. "She and another woman pulled up to the house not long after the second man left."

"Can you tell me anything about the other woman?"

Erna went silent. Then she said, "If they find out . . ."

"No one is going to hurt you."

"You didn't see his eyes."

"Who?"

"I can't," she said and left the room.

CHAPTER 37

I found her staring out her kitchen window several moments later. A tea kettle was whistling on the stove but she was oblivious to the sound. I quietly removed the screaming kettle from the element and turned off the stove. It must have been the quiet that alerted her to my presence because she started speaking almost immediately.

"Shelagh had flowers and an overnight bag. She knocked on the door a couple of times and let herself in. She looked . . . nervous. Kept checking to see if anyone was watching. She didn't see me. Not then."

Erna never took her gaze from the window. It was like she was watching the scene unfold now, this very minute, just as she had all those years ago. "When she came back out, she had changed her clothes. The other woman was still in the car and Shelagh had to help her get out. She wasn't well. She wouldn't have been able to stand if it weren't for Shelagh. The two of them went into the house and that's when . . . the man . . . arrived. I thought for a moment it was Olivia's husband, he was so big."

She was clearly terrified of whoever this man was. Even his memory seemed to have some power over her. I waited for her to continue.

"He brought a tree and a shovel around the side of the house."

"A tree?"

"In a pot. Maybe it was just a tall plant but it looked like a

214

tree. A young one. Shelagh came out of the house and the two of them spoke for several minutes in the driveway. They appeared to argue. The man looked like he was going to leave and that's when he saw me." She fought to keep her breath. "Oh, Ms. James, if you could have seen the anger. The rage."

"You're doing great, Erna," I said. "What happened after they saw you?"

"I hid. I turned off the lights and watched from the small window in the front door. He never took his gaze off this house."

"The woman, was it Marjorie?" Jeffers asked over the phone.

"It must have been. Who else could it have been? Erna said she didn't see the woman's face. In fact, she said the woman was covered up. But the woman's size matches and Erna said she saw a few strands of dark hair escape from the covering, just like Marjorie had in her mug shot. It had to have been her."

"Okay, let's say it was. What else?"

"She said the man kept shaking his head while he and Shelagh were arguing, like he was refusing to do something. Eventually, he threw his hands in the air and they went into the house."

"Mm-hm."

I could hear Jeffers rustling papers. "Are you listening to me?"

"Yeah. Go on."

"*You* asked me to start from the beginning. If you only wanted the good stuff, you should have said so."

"I'm listening!"

When I'd called, Jeffers had just passed his second hour in the archives with nothing to show for it. He was quickly losing patience. And faith.

"What then?" he asked.

"I think that's when the real Olivia was murdered and

Marjorie was beaten beyond recognition."

"Bella, focus on the interrogation. What did Erna say happened after they went into the house?"

"It wasn't an interrogation."

"What did she say?"

"Nothing. They went into the house and then nothing. She said she watched for a bit longer then stopped. A half hour or so later she heard a car door slam. She went to her door and saw the man leaving. Shelagh followed shortly thereafter and about a half hour after that, the police arrived."

"According to the police report, Erna Weins was the one who called the police. She's on the record as saying she heard Olivia arguing with someone. She heard some crashing and screaming. She said Olivia was begging her attacker to stop."

"I know! But get this. Erna told me she never gave a statement. She didn't call the police. She never said a word to the police about that night until you called her a few weeks ago."

I heard a stack of pages hit the surface of a tabletop. I now had Jeffers' undivided attention.

"Bella," he said, "when I spoke with Erna Weins, she told me almost word for word what was in the police file."

"That's what Shelagh Worthy told her to say."

"You've lost me."

"Apparently, Shelagh went by Erna's house a few days after the fact. Wove some story about Duck having been Olivia's attacker. Gave quite a graphic account about what had happened. She kept insisting Erna must have heard something. So much so that by the time her storytelling was done, Erna actually believed she *had* heard the begging and screaming."

"Okay, but that still doesn't explain how it got in the police report."

"The next part of the story was almost too much for me to fathom. The man . . . the man who was with Shelagh . . . the one who brought the tree . . . when the police arrived on the scene, Erna said he was there."

"What do you mean, there? Like he came back to watch? Oh, Jesus, Bella, are you telling me he's a cop?"

CHAPTER 38

Jeffers hung up before I had a chance to tell him of the threats Shelagh had made to Erna and the payoffs, disguised as charitable donations, she had given in exchange for Erna's silence. The news that a police officer could have been involved in such a heinous crime hit Jeffers hard.

Most cops swore by their duty to uphold the law, but I knew there was a long and unfortunate history of some who believed themselves to be above it.

The day had taken its toll on me. I opened a bottle of red, put a bowl of leftover chili in the microwave, and called Natalie. She picked up on the fourth ring, sounding out of breath.

"Are you okay?" I asked

"Yeah, I'm just getting in. Heard the phone from outside. I was going to call you. You got a great review in the *Globe*."

Most actors claim not to care about reviews. They're lying.

"So I've heard. I still haven't seen it."

"Zack cut it out. I'll send it to you."

"Great," I said through a mouthful of steaming chili.

I remembered how Terri-Mae had collected every review, every article that had ever been printed about me. Even the sordid ones about my relationship with Rich Arborall. She insisted I send her everything. Rather than actually having a conversation with her, I had obliged. I felt a tightening in my throat and closed my eyes.

"Are *you* all right?" Natalie asked.

"Yes," I said, appreciating her sensitivity.

"So, how'd it go?"

I told her all about the glitz and glam of the opening and about how wonderful Olivia had been.

"According to the review," Natalie said, "Olivia wasn't the only one."

"Reviews are just one person's opinion."

"But it's still nice to know that that one person thought you were the brightest star to hit the Shaw Festival stage in almost a decade."

"It doesn't say that. Does it?"

"It says, and I quote, 'Bella James' portrayal of the title character is, in a word, magnificent.' "

Embarrassed, I said, "I'll read it myself." She kept reading. "Natalie!"

She continued her recitation through giggles of self-congratulation. She knew she was driving me crazy. I held the phone away from my ear and started singing a chorus of random *la-la-la*s. Moustache harrumphed at all the noise then let out a series of *woofs* as a knock sounded at the front door.

"Natalie, hold on." I put the phone on the counter and left Natalie and the review to entertain one another without me.

The landing was empty when I opened the door, save for a bouquet of flowers. The bouquet was absolutely gorgeous—a mix of hot pink gerberas, orange bi-color roses, and a spray of green button chrysanthemums. I sunk my nose into their beautiful scent. Natalie, thank goodness, had finished her recital by the time I got back on the phone.

"Sorry about that," I said, taking in another breath of the sweet aroma. "Somebody just delivered some flowers."

"At this hour? Ooh, an admirer. Who are they from?"

I looked at the clock on the stove and blinked as the digits danced wildly. "What time is it?"

"Bella, are you okay? You sound weird."

"I'm fine," I said, slurring slightly.

I opened the envelope that was taped to the plastic wrapping and pulled out a copy of the review Natalie had been reading. The phrase "Is Bella James the next Olivia Childries?" was highlighted in bright yellow and the photo accompanying the article was one of Olivia and me in a scene from the beginning of the play's third act. My face had been replaced with the drawing of a skull.

"Oh my God," I managed.

"Bel?"

My heart began to race. My vision blurred and I fought the urge to vomit. I looked at the flowers and my mind was instantly flooded with voices:

Erna: "Well, the flowers for one thing. It seemed like one delivery after another."

Peter: "She was out of it. Incoherent. There were flowers everywhere."

Duck: "House smelled of flowers."

"It was the flowers," I mumbled into the phone.

"What? Bella, what's going on? I can't understand you!"

I reached out to steady myself against the counter and knocked a glass into the sink, where it shattered. The noise attracted Moustache who came over to investigate. My brain appealed for Natalie to "tell Jeffers," but my mouth was unable to fully form the words and the plea came out resembling something one of the adults in a Charlie Brown cartoon might have said.

"Bella!" Natalie kept screaming my name.

Moustache was jumping up on me, barking.

The voices in my head were yelling over one another.

My eyelids grew heavy. I couldn't . . . keep . . . them . . .

CHAPTER 39

I knew I was outside when I finally came to, but had no idea where I was or how long I had been unconscious. There was something covering my head and face. I tried to move my mouth but it had been taped shut. Further exploration told me my wrists and ankles had also been bound. I screamed through the tape and began to writhe on the ground, kicking my legs as hard as I could. A hand pulled the hood off my head, taking with it a few pieces of hair, and I winced at the sting.

"Oh, good, you're awake," said Shelagh Worthy, who stood over me in what I guessed to be a pair of Duck's overalls. Although she had rolled the cuffs, the outfit swallowed her up and made her look like she'd been shrunken. Garden gloves protected her pie-making hands and a smear of dirt ran across her brow. A lawn mower was idling by the garden shed, no doubt to conceal the noise, and a shovel lay not too far from me. A mound of dirt sat on the lawn a few feet away and I recognized the hole that had been emptied. It had been home to the real Olivia's bones.

"I wanted *you* to know your fate," Shelagh said. "I took pity on Livvie. Gave her enough to *keep* her unconscious but you . . . you just couldn't leave it alone, could you?"

I had seen those eyes before. In the kitchen at Olivia's Easter bash. There was a wildness in them that had disturbed me then but terrified me now. I moaned.

"Ms. James, I'm really sorry but I don't have time to listen to you beg," she said, slipping back into her sweet drawl. "You see, as much as I wanted her dead, I didn't want Livvie to suffer. I mean, goodness, she was my best friend. But there comes a time when enough is enough. You know?"

She looked at me deeply, appealing for understanding. Or sympathy.

"Ever since we were children, I had to stand by and watch Livvie get everything," she whined. "The good looks, the stardom, the perfect husband. And then there was the baby!"

The word "baby" was uttered with a bitterness that caught me off guard and a whimper escaped me. Shelagh looked at me as if seeing me for the first time. Her eyes were cold.

"Didn't you know about the baby?" she asked.

I shook my head as a tear rolled down my cheek. With the mention of the baby, Shelagh's whole demeanor had changed, and I went from terrified to petrified.

"Of course you didn't know," she scoffed. "No one knew. I was the only one with whom she shared her—happy—news. She was going to tell Duck that night. Had it all planned. Champagne, a fancy dinner, lingerie. I knew I had to do something before that happened. If I had to endure watching their happy little family bloom . . . it was the *one* thing I wanted."

She picked up my feet, dragged me closer to the hole and put me down with my back to its edge.

"Drugging Olivia was the easy part," she continued. "Small doses of chloroform on the flowers took care of that. My granddaddy was a doctor in the military. Never threw anything away. A visit to his garage and a few innocent questions and I had everything I needed. Poor old man had no idea what I was getting at. He thought I was just interested in hearing about his glory days. It's so much easier nowadays with the internet. Then, of course, I had to figure out how to get her alone in the house. That was trickier. I called Peter, pretending to be Olivia, and asked him over so he would be there when Duck returned home. Duck hated the man. He tolerated him for Livvie's sake, but if he had the chance to make himself scarce whenever Peter was around, he took it. I knew as soon as Duck saw Peter, he would find some excuse to leave.

"Peter carried a torch for Olivia. That was one of the reasons Duck hated him so much. But never, in my right mind, would I have anticipated that Peter would take things so far. My goodness. I figured he would've simply left when he saw Olivia was unwell."

She was positively gleeful at this, and I felt my stomach turn over at the thought that she could relate the story of her best friend's rape with so little shame.

"Duck was absolutely beside himself at the sight," she prattled on. "And it gave me the idea to fabricate a torrid affair. Duck didn't dispute it when I told him. Heck, he had just seen it with his own eyes!"

She stared at me a long while before speaking again. "Anyway," she finally said, "since Olivia died with her baby, I thought it only fair that you should do the same. A perfect encore."

She shoved me with her foot, turning me at an angle that gave me a clear view of the hole's contents. I let out as much of a scream as the tape allowed and began to thrash wildly against my bindings. Moustache lay at the bottom of the hole, all four legs stretched out to one side, as if in a peaceful slumber.

"Oh, stop it!" she ordered, giving me a swift kick to the ribs. "He's fine. Just unconscious. I had to give him something to stop that incessant barking. Of course, if that antifreeze had done its job . . . but then I wouldn't have the pleasure of watching you die together."

She gave me another shove into the hole. I wrenched my body so I wouldn't land on top of Moustache. Since my hands had been tied in front, I was able to scramble over to him and nuzzle my face against his. Shelagh had been telling the truth. He was alive.

"How sweet," Shelagh said. "Although, if he hadn't dug up those bones in the first place, you wouldn't be in this position." She began shoveling dirt back into the hole. "And if there hadn't been a baby I might have been able to keep going. I might have been able to accept Olivia's charmed life but, you see, I had been trying and trying and trying to get pregnant."

Each "trying" was accompanied by a fresh pile of dirt. There was a brief respite as she wiped her brow. I took the opportunity to shake whatever I could off me and Moustache.

"I was devastated when the doctor told me I would never be able to conceive and when Olivia told me about her baby . . . well . . . that was it."

She used the shovel to help her balance as she squatted at the hole's edge and looked down at me and said, "It wasn't until I met Marjorie that the idea struck me. She looked a bit like Olivia. Not nearly as pretty, of course. All I had to do was make her believe her husband was beating down the shelter door to get at her. Poor thing was almost paralyzed with fear. As long as I 'kept him away,' she was putty in my hands. Pathetic soul. But look at her now. If it hadn't have been for me, lord knows what would have happened to her. I saved her."

If she only knew how Marjorie really felt.

"And I got the man! Me! Ended up with the perfect husband after all, didn't I?"

I heard a sadness coloring her words. In the little time I had spent with Duck, I knew Olivia had been his only real love and I guessed Shelagh knew it, too, in her heart.

"And then your dog comes along and digs up the bones and you start playing Nancy Drew and everything starts going to hell!"

Her shoveling became more and more aggressive. I managed to form a little pocket of air around my nose with one hand and pulled Moustache on top of me so I could do the same for him. I didn't know what good it would do, but it was all I could think of.

"Oh, and in case you're expecting some miraculous rescue, I've already left a message for your stage manager, telling her you're under the weather and didn't think you could do the show tomorrow night."

What was left of my rational mind called her bluff until I remembered she'd gotten my phone number off of Olivia's contact sheet and could have done what she claimed.

"As for this little grave here, by the time I'm done it won't look any different from how the police left it. No one will think to look here."

One more pile of dirt obscured my face. My pocket of air held strong and I could feel Moustache's warm exhales in my other hand.

"It didn't have to end up like this," Shelagh said. "You should have left well enough alone."

I felt the weight of the dirt increase on top of me, every ounce crushing my hopes. I expected my life to start flashing before my eyes. I waited for it. I waited for important people and events to act as a comfort in my final moments. But nothing. No smiling faces or happy memories, nothing but me, lying in my grave with my hand cradling my dog's nose.

And silence.

CHAPTER 40

"Welcome back," a man's voice said. "We thought we lost you."

My eyes fought against the brightness of the light. I was on my back and the light was directly overhead. I tried to speak but the sound was muffled by whatever was around my mouth. I brought a hand up to remove the contraption, but was stopped by the man who had been speaking.

"No, you need to leave that right where it is." The man stood over me, holding my hands in his own. "It's an oxygen mask. It's there to help you breathe a little easier, all right?"

I nodded.

He had soft hands and a calm way of speaking. And he was handsome. Chiseled features, short dark hair, athletic build. I managed to turn my gaze from the man's face and take in the rest of my surroundings.

"Ms. James, my name is R.J. I'm a paramedic. We're in an ambulance. We're taking you to the hospital."

I nodded again. I was shivering.

"Do you remember what happened?" R.J. asked.

I lifted my head and looked down at myself. A thermal blanket covered most of my body, but one of my arms was exposed and fitted with an I.V. The skin was filthy, save for the area in which the needle had been inserted. My fingernails were caked with dirt. I stared at my hand for a long time. I remembered . . . holding something. My hand fumbled at the mask, trapping my words.

"My dog," I managed to get out before R.J reaffixed the mask. I felt tears stream down my dirty cheeks.

"Ms. James, you're all right now. You're going to be fine."

Clearly he hadn't heard what I'd said. I made another attempt at the mask. I shook my head wildly and fought against his efforts to restrain me. Our struggle lasted only a few short moments before I felt a warm sensation flow through my entire body. I looked back at my hand, my last connection to Moustache. Somehow, it didn't feel at all connected to the rest of my body.

R.J. was saying something to me, but I couldn't understand his words. I felt as if I was being submerged in a warm bath. My eyelids grew heavy as I fell deeper and deeper into the bath's warm embrace.

I woke up in a hospital room. Jeffers was asleep in a chair across from me. The oxygen mask was gone, but the I.V. remained. I had been cleaned of the dirt. But not of the memories.

"Jeffers?" I whispered. It hurt to speak. "Jeffers," I said again, a little louder.

"Hey," he said, rushing to my side and perching himself on the edge of the bed. Relief spread across his face. "How are you feeling?"

"Moustache?"

"He's fine. I had the guys call the animal hospital as soon as we found you. One of the paramedics administered first aid. Do you know they give animals CPR through their nose? They have to completely cover the nose with their mouth! I don't know that I'd want a dog's nose in my mouth. I mean they're always sniffing other dogs' butts and licking their, uh, private parts."

The look on my face must have told him to get on with it.

"He was breathing on his own by the time the vet arrived. Your friend, Dr. We're Not Talking About It."

I rolled my eyes.

"The doc assured me Moustache would make a complete recovery," Jeffers continued. "He said he'd bring him to the clinic to get cleaned up, warmed up, and started on some fluids. He promised to call if anything changed but said you should be able to pick him up in the morning, if you're up to it."

I nodded, smiled, and let out the breath I didn't know I was holding. "It was Shelagh." The words sounded raspy and they grated against my vocal cords as I spoke.

"I know. We got her. She's at the station. Hasn't admitted to anything yet, but it's a matter of time."

"She drugged me. There was something on the flowers. That's how she drugged Olivia, too."

"We didn't find any flowers. She must have taken them with her when she cleaned up. But the doctor ordered a tox screen, so it should show up there."

"Erna said—"

"Bella, this can all wait." He clasped my hand. "We have plenty of time to talk about this, but right now I want to know about you. How are *you*?"

"I'm okay," I said, giving his hand a squeeze. "I think."

"You had some mild hypothermia and dehydration. The doctors also ran some tests to determine if there was any damage to the brain. An MRI or CT or something. I called the theatre, told them you'd been involved in an accident and wouldn't be available for the show tomorrow."

"What? Why?"

"They said your understudy had already been informed. Although how they knew that—"

"Shelagh. She made a similar call. Wanted to be sure no one would come looking for me. Give me your phone," I said. Jeffers obliged and I punched in my stage manager's number.

I had no idea what time it was and didn't care. No actor, unless he or she is dead or dying, wants an understudy to go on for them.

After four rings the answering machine clicked in. True to form, Caitlin's outgoing recording was one long apology. I got the beep and left a long message assuring her that I was perfectly fine and would be doing the show the following evening.

"My understudy is atrocious," I said matter-of-factly after I'd hung up. "There's no way I'm going to let her go on. Sometimes people don't bother to read the program insert, and I don't want them to mistake her for me."

Jeffers stared at me.

"I'm not being a catty diva, Jeffers. In most cases understudies are more than capable of doing the job. Unfortunately, this is not one of those cases."

"Jesus, it's just for one night!"

I imagined he was close to using what would become his angry dad voice, and was a little surprised by his vehemence. "She can't seem to get a handle on Shaw's language," I said, "and because she doesn't even have a small part in the show, copying my performance is not an option. I'll be fine by tomorrow."

"You were buried alive!"

"Jeffers?" I reached out my arm to him.

He kept his distance but faced me head on. "I thought you were dead," he said, quietly. "There was so much dirt. And I had to dig with my hands."

There was a heaviness in my chest as I noticed, for the first time, how dirty his clothes were. He had been the one to find me. He had been the one who pulled me out of the ground.

"Jeffers, how did you know I was there?"

He brought a hand to his face and when he took it away I could see that his eyes were red. "I love you, Bella. I love you like I love my sisters. I have three of them and I know what it feels like to love them and that's how I feel about you." He took my hands in his and kissed my forehead.

I felt just as fondly toward Jeffers, but putting words to my feelings was still a work in progress. "How did you know I was there?" I repeated.

A knock on the door kept Jeffers from answering my question. Skip Raines stuck his head in. "How much longer? I want to get this over with."

"What's he doing here?" I asked, not bothering to disguise my disdain.

"He," Jeffers began with some reluctance, "is pretty much responsible for saving your life."

"I don't understand. I thought you said *you* found me."

"I did. I'm the one who dug. I'm the one who pulled you out. *He* told me where to find you."

"What do you mean?" I turned my gaze on Raines. "What does he mean you told him where to find me? How did you know?"

Raines' massive frame filled the doorway. His shoulders slouched and his eyes refused to meet mine. His usual bluster had been reined in, but just barely. I could feel the venom pumping though his body.

"Oh my God," I whispered as the realization sunk in.

Raines turned his eyes on me and clenched a fist. The same eyes that had been haunting Erna Weins for years. The same fists that had obliterated Marjorie Adelman's face.

"It was you!"

CHAPTER 41

"I didn't know about Olivia," Raines said. I shook my head in disbelief. "I didn't," he growled. "Not until you and Jeffers said so in Morris' office."

I remembered how Raines had looked like he was going to vomit as Jeffers and I shared our findings about the bones with the Inspector. I looked to Jeffers. He nodded.

"I found a document in the archives linking Shelagh and Raines," he said.

"Linking how?"

"Raines is Shelagh's ex-husband. We were in the midst of a little chat when Natalie's call came in."

"Natalie?" I asked, confused. "My Natalie?"

"Yep. She called, frantic. She said you two had been talking when you suddenly started rambling on in gibberish. She thought you were having a stroke. She managed to catch my name and something about flowers, but couldn't make out much else. I sent the paramedics to your place. I expected they'd find you somewhere in the house. It was Raines who knew different."

I raised an eyebrow to Raines. He returned the look with eyes that warned of fury looming. "I called Shelagh after Jeffers told me he suspected she was involved in Olivia's murder," he said.

"Before I went down to the archives," Jeffers interjected, "as per Inspector Morris' orders."

"You called to alert her?" I said to Raines.

"I thought she would leave town or something," he said. "When Jeffers got that call from your friend, I knew she was behind it. I knew what she was trying to do."

"Recreate Olivia's murder. I thought you didn't know about the murder," I challenged.

Raines sank into one of the hospital chairs, resigned to the fact that he was not going to leave without telling me the whole story. "After that stunt you two pulled in Morris' office, I called Shelagh:

"Olivia's dead! Those bones they found at Olivia's old house were Olivia's!"

"Don't be ridiculous. Olivia is perfectly fine."

"There's proof, Shelagh! Dental records. Who was that woman?"

"Skip, I—"

"Shelagh, you asked me to put the fists to Olivia for some crackpot reason. And I did. But the woman I . . . did that to . . . wasn't Olivia was it?"

"No."

"They think whoever this woman is, killed Olivia and has been parading around as her ever since. Is that true? Shelagh? Did—that—woman—kill—Olivia?"

"Skip, calm down."

"Don't tell me to calm down! I put myself on the case, Shelagh! When I heard a body had been found on that property I knew it couldn't be a coincidence! I have tried to dead end this investigation! I have put stops up at every turn because I had a feeling those bones were connected to that night!!! I have broken the law for you!"

"You didn't do it for me! You did it to protect your own ass!"

"Dammit, woman!"

"Look, I'll take care of it. Just keep doing whatever you have to do to stall this investigation."

"From what I know, you're not even on the radar. But, so help me, Shelagh, I will not go down for this without taking you with me."

"She asked you to beat up Olivia?" I was sickened at the thought.

"Remember how Shelagh was a client at Mercy Lodge," Jeffers said, "before she started to volunteer?"

"Of course." I looked at Raines. "This was behavior you were all too familiar with. Hitting women. So when she asked you to destroy her best friend's face, you just *did* it?"

"It wasn't like that."

"Then how was it? Because I can't imagine any reason good enough to do what you did."

I looked at Jeffers, who had his gaze fixed on Raines.

Raines brought one of his deadly hands to his face and rubbed his eyes. He let out a long exhale. "Shelagh told me Olivia wanted out of her marriage. Said Duck had been abusive, which I thought was a crock. That man wouldn't hurt a flea and he adored Olivia. But Shelagh said that was all for show. That Olivia had finally had enough, but Duck wouldn't let her go. Shelagh said indisputable proof of his violence was the only way."

"Duck never hurt Olivia," I said.

"I know that now!"

"So Shelagh called the only man she knew who could get the job done, right?"

Raines stared at the floor. "Not exactly."

"Then what, exactly?"

"Shelagh asked me to come to Olivia's . . . that night . . . to drop off a tree she had bought. Her car wasn't big enough and we were still, sort of, speaking at that point."

"What does that mean?"

"We were going through a divorce and were in the process of working out the details."

"Okay, so what about the tree?"

"She said it was a gift. Something about new life and growth and I don't know what. Shelagh was always kind of flighty like that."

"Then what?"

"Shelagh's car was already there. I figured she and Olivia were inside and I knew the tree was supposed to be a surprise, so I brought it around the side of the house. I was coming back to my car when Shelagh came out:

"Skip, there's one more thing I need you to do."

"You said this would only take a minute."

"I need you to beat up Olivia."

"Are you out of your mind!"

"Skip, listen. It's what I told you. It's about getting the proof she needs to leave Duck. Livvie's completely on board. In fact, it was her idea. I've already given her a sedative. She won't feel a thing."

"What are you looking at, you nosy old bat?"

"Shhh, it's just one of the neighbors."

"Yeah, a neighbor who can identify us."

"No one is going to be able to connect us to this. I will go over there later and straighten things out. I might even be able to use her to our advantage. But right now we are wasting time. If Livvie's drugs wear off—"

"Shelagh, I'm not doing this!"

"Yes, you are, Skip, and let me tell you why. I have kept your abuse of me a secret because of how it would affect your position. I promised you my silence so you would let me go. Not even the people at the shelter know who I am married to. But I would be more than happy to have a chat with your superior. And my divorce lawyer. You've given me bruises, and broken bones, and death threats. Now I am asking you to give me one more thing. And then we're even."

"Would it really have been that bad?" I said. "The department knowing? I mean, surely you're not the first officer to ever hit his wife."

"I was in line for a promotion," Raines said. "My record was clean and that's how it needed to stay. An assault charge would have derailed everything."

Whether he meant it or not, there was shame in his admission and that, and only that, gave him some humanity.

"So obviously you agreed," I said.

"The woman I thought was Olivia was lying on the living room floor, unconscious. Shelagh told me to keep the lights off, probably so I wouldn't see who the woman really was. She told me to focus on the woman's face then she left me alone. When I'd finished, I found Shelagh out back planting the tree."

"She was burying Olivia and using the tree to disguise the grave."

"I didn't know that then. Shelagh said she was going to call it in to the police. She said it would be easier to control the situation if I were the one leading the case, so I got cleaned up, left, and waited for the call to come in. Made sure I was one of the first to respond."

"That lines up with the forty minutes we couldn't account for," Jeffers put in.

"And the notes?" I asked.

"Shelagh told me what to write but to hold off submitting it. A day or so later she told me about the neighbor. It was easy to add that in."

My mind whirled. "And now?"

"Now," said Jeffers, "we're off to see the Inspector."

Raines rose from his seat, clearly exhausted from having already relived the experience twice, first with Jeffers and then for my benefit. I could see by the pallor of his cheeks that the idea of having to suffer the ordeal again in front of Inspector Morris was making him physically ill. The only sympathy I had for him stemmed from the fact that he had finally made a good decision by coming clean and saving my life.

"Did you get the promotion?" I asked as Raines filled the

doorway on his way out. "The promotion you were in line for? The promotion you were protecting when you brutalized Marjorie Adelman?"

He gave a sardonic smile. "No."

CHAPTER 42

I was in a light doze when a young nurse stuck her head in.

"Ms. James? I'm so sorry to wake you but your doctor is here and would like a minute. May I send him in?"

"Of course," I said sleepily.

She smiled kindly and signaled to someone unseen. Dr. Gorgeous edged by the nurse, into the room, giving her a nod of thanks. She lowered her face to hide her blushing and retreated into the hallway.

"You're not a people doctor," I teased.

"I may have neglected to mention that part. I have something to show you." He pulled out his phone and perched on the side of the bed.

His phone showed Moustache sleeping soundly, half his body under a flowered blanket. He, too, had been cleaned and, like me, had been fitted with an I.V. I looked up at Dr. Gorgeous, tears streaming down my face, too overwhelmed to speak.

"I knew you must be worried," Dr. Gorgeous said.

I nodded, not taking my gaze off the screen. He leaned over and adjusted the volume so that I could, albeit barely, hear my pup's faint snores.

"He is going to be perfectly fine," Dr. Gorgeous assured me. "He was dehydrated and a little disoriented, but he snapped out of that pretty quickly. I had him on a breathing tube for a bit. I don't know if anyone told you, but one of the paramedics had to perform CPR."

"I know."

"By the time I got to your place, Moustache was breathing on his own but it was labored. I wanted to relieve some of the pressure on his heart. That's why I put the tube in. He's breathing normally now and there doesn't appear to be any other damage. All his motor and cognitive skills are good and he had a hearty appetite."

The video had ended by this time and I was staring at a still image. "Thank you," I said, clutching the phone to my heart before returning it.

"How are you?"

"Breathing on my own," I began, mirroring the vet's assessment of Moustache. "Mentally and physically fine. Not much of an appetite, though."

"Well, that's good because all I have are a few milk bones and a liver treat."

He smiled and I managed a laugh. After a moment, his face grew serious and he inhaled as if he was going to say something, but reconsidered. I didn't know what the police had told him, but I could only imagine he must have questions.

"I don't know how much you know," I said, carefully.

"Right now I know everything I need to. You and Moustache are going to be perfectly fine. And as your doctor," he said with mock authority, "I think you should follow Moustache's example and get some sleep. You must be exhausted. He'll be ready for you in the morning."

For the second time since I moved in, my little cottage was surrounded with police tape. Mercifully, someone, presumably the police, had filled the hole in the backyard. Moustache sniffed around the area as usual, lifting his leg and kicking up dirt, completely oblivious to the fact that not even twenty-four hours earlier, we had been left to suffocate beneath the same earth.

Every now and then he would abandon his exploration and run to me, wagging his entire body, putting his head between my knees for a scratch, and then running off to uncover the next great smell.

Dr. Gorgeous had not been at the clinic when I picked Moustache up, but he had left a note saying there'd be no charge for the dog's care.

I'd been given permission for Moustache to stay in my dressing room during the show. Jeffers had been keeping me apprised of things all day and I knew there was no further threat to us, but I wanted Moustache close.

Jeffers said Shelagh was maintaining her innocence in both Olivia's murder and her attempt at mine. Whether she eventually confessed or not didn't concern Jeffers. My statement along with Raines' testimony and that of Erna Weins was enough to see to it that charges were laid.

Evidently Raines was cooperating fully, but Jeffers had failed to fill me in on what had transpired during the meeting with Inspector Morris. I highly doubted Raines would be allowed an honorable discharge after all he had done, despite his last minute decision to do the right thing. I found the man to be completely insufferable and I hated that he'd played such a pivotal role in saving my life, but I knew things would have turned out differently without him. As a result, I found myself hoping his fall would be cushioned. Just a bit.

Olivia was sitting in my dressing room when Moustache and I arrived at the theatre. Moustache ran to her and allowed her to pet him for a split second before dashing into the hallway to make the rounds. Olivia watched him go with sad eyes. I waited for her to speak.

"I had a phone call today from your friend Andre Jeffers. He told me what happened. My God, Bella, are you all right?"

239

"I'm fine."

She reached out her hands to me. A glance into the hallway showed Moustache's rear end disappearing into Jarod Riley's dressing room. Jarod was not a lot of things, but he was an avid dog lover and I knew Moustache would be fine. I took one of Olivia's outstretched hands and settled into the chair across from her.

"What are you doing here?" she asked. "Why on earth didn't you take the night off?"

"Would you really rather have done the show with my understudy?"

"Oh, my God!" Olivia exclaimed.

We shared a laugh.

"Did Jeffers tell you everything?" I asked.

Tears formed in her eyes. "As much as he was able to piece together."

"So you know you're not at all responsible for—"

"Yes, I know. I'm a victim of this whole mess. The same as you. The same as . . . Olivia."

"But?"

"We talked about Marjorie."

"And?"

"Bella, I've had a beautiful life as Olivia. It has been by no means perfect, but on the whole I've been very fortunate. But this was not the life that was intended for me. I was destined for something far less charmed. How can I consider myself a victim when I've been so blessed?"

"Olivia, you've had your own share of suffering. Shelagh terrorized you as Marjorie into believing your husband was trying to kill you. She manipulated you to think she was the only person in the world who could keep you safe, and then she put you in the hands of a man who did far worse than Lance Adelman ever could."

"But, mercifully, I don't remember that."

"That doesn't mean it didn't happen. How many years did you spend feeling like a stranger in your own body? And when you finally discovered your true identity, regained some memories, Shelagh stole them from you again by playing with your medication. You've spent a lot of this charmed life, as you call it, depressed and confused and frustrated. And maybe it's true that the life you were given was better than the one you were taken from, but Marjorie was on the road to recovery. Who knows what she could have aspired to? What life she could have made for herself? You've suffered, Olivia. Maybe more than anyone."

She brought both hands to her face and cried quietly behind them, then let out a shaky breath. "Andre told me the department is not going to go public with any of this."

I was surprised but relieved. I was sure the story would turn the theatre world on its ear and I wasn't sure how Olivia would fare. There were bound to be those who would overlook Shelagh's involvement entirely and herald Olivia as the merry murderer and identity thief. I was glad to know her revival would be allowed to happen in some privacy and that she would have time to heal. If she could.

"What are you going to do?" I asked.

"Finish the season like I planned. I'll let the theatre fête me and my years and then send me off into the wings. I may have been riding on someone else's coattails, but I've given a lot of myself to this company and I'm proud of what I've accomplished."

"You deserve every ounce of attention and admiration you're going to get."

"Then I'm going to try to reconnect with the woman I once was so she and the woman I am now can co-exist. I've stopped taking any medication. Dr. Lin said that whatever memories

were being blocked by Shelagh's interference should rematerial-
ize."

"I'm happy for you," I said.

"Ladies and gentlemen, this is your half-hour call," Caitlin
said over the intercom.

"But first, I guess, we've got a show to do," Olivia said, smiling as she stood to go.

"If you want me along for any part of your recovery, I'm
here."

She took my hand and kissed it before pulling me into an
embrace. I hugged her hard, thankful that this woman, whom I
had come to love, was not the monster I had initially believed.

"It might be a bit of a bumpy ride," she cautioned.

"I've been on one or two of those," I said. "I'll be fine."

CHAPTER 43

Moustache was curled up on Manda's robe when I got back to the dressing room after the curtain came down. How he had managed to get it off the rack, I had no idea, but I inwardly applauded his feat. He had arranged the robe into a little purple mound and when he saw me, he flopped over onto his side and lifted a leg to expose his belly for a scratch. Once satisfied, he gave up his pillow and, after a quick stretch, moved to dance in front of the door, itching to get out and say his farewells.

For the second time that night, I watched his rear end disappear into Jarod Riley's dressing room. My dog clearly did not share my taste in men.

I picked Manda's dressing gown up off the floor and tried, futilely, to smooth out some of the wrinkles. A card fell from the pocket. It said "Thanks for the tickets. Have a great Opening Night." It was from Dr. Gorgeous. The message was innocuous enough, but I was reading it with green eyes, which made it seem far more provocative.

I bunched the robe into a ball before hanging it back on the rack and huffed as I gave the card one last read before replacing it in the richly embroidered pocket.

The show was one of the best Olivia and I had done. It had felt good. I felt free. I was no longer the detective sharing the stage with a woman who was heavily shrouded in my own suspicion. This time she had been the great Olivia Childries and I had been the actress lucky enough to share scenes with her.

"I think this belongs to you," Jarod Riley said as he ushered Moustache into my room.

"Thanks," I said. "I hope he wasn't a bother."

"He can visit any time," Jarod said, giving Moustache one final scratch behind the ears. "We're heading over to the Angel to get a drink. He's welcome to stay in my car if you want to join us."

"Thanks, but I think we're going to head home tonight."

"Well, then, I'll see you tomorrow." He turned to go then stopped. "Bella, is everything okay?"

"What do you mean?"

"I heard there was an ambulance and police by your place last night. Your understudy called me in a panic, wanting to run lines."

The police had promised Olivia things would be kept as private as possible, which meant only a handful of people really knew what had transpired the night before. I was only too happy to do my part in keeping it that way.

"It was just a silly little accident," I said.

I was in the midst of trying to untangle myself from Moustache's leash when Adam stuck his head out of the passenger window of a car.

"I hope you're coming for a drink," he said. "You were amazing tonight! It's on me!"

"Not tonight. I'm already spoken for," I said, indicating Moustache, whose neck was at an odd angle as I worked the knot that the leash had entwined us in.

"He's right. You were amazing."

I turned toward the voice and saw a man sitting on one of the benches that were outside the entrance into the box office.

"Mr. Worthy?"

"Olivia would have said that you were better than she had been."

"Mr. Worthy, what are you doing here?"

"Duck. Please."

"Duck," I said, the name sounding strange in my mouth. "What are you doing here?" I freed Moustache and me from the entanglement and joined Duck on the bench.

"I had to see her for myself," he said.

"Olivia?" I saw him flinch at the mention of her name. "I'm sorry. I meant—"

"It's all right," he said and folded his burly arms across his chest.

We sat for a moment in silence. Me looking at him, him looking at the stars, and Moustache, sensing that this might take a while, settling at my feet. I opened my mouth to speak but before I could he said, "I brought some things for Shelagh. The police called early this morning. I thought they were going to tell me they had finally arrested that Adelman woman for Livvie's murder. I never expected . . ."

He brought his hands to his knees and straightened. I took the opportunity to reach out and take one of his hands in mine. He squeezed my fingers, much more gently than I ever would have believed he could with hands of his size.

"Mr. Worthy . . . Duck, I am so sorry."

"I didn't want to see her. Shelagh. Didn't think I could is more like it. Don't know if I'll ever be able to. Or want to. But I still couldn't bear the thought of her sitting in that place without a decent nightgown."

I felt my chest tighten and fought back tears. My very core was struck by this man's sensitivity even in the midst of his own personal nightmare.

"It's funny, you know. I never particularly cared for Shelagh. I put up with her because she was Olivia's best friend. But after

Olivia—after the divorce—Shelagh would come by with a cas-serole or pie or something. Took to doing a bit of the housework. Told me she was worried about me. Wanted to make sure I was okay. She started coming by more and more, and, I don't know how it happened, but one day she just stayed. I guess I had got-ten so used to her being there that instead of asking her to leave, I asked her to marry me. I cared for her, but my heart could never love her. Not like she wanted.

"Anyway, I needed to see for myself, once and for all, the woman who calls herself Olivia. I needed to know, for certain, she was not my Livvie."

"And?"

"I knew the second she walked on stage." His eyes filled with tears.

"Duck, you need to know that . . . Marjorie . . . didn't know anything about what had happened to Olivia. She was not involved in any way."

"The police told me everything. And I feel terrible for that woman, to be perfectly honest. What Shelagh did to her is . . . there are no words."

I nodded. "May I ask what you're planning to do now?"

"I'm going to take my wife and . . . my baby . . . and bury them where I can be close to them." He pulled a handkerchief out of his pocket to dab at his eyes and wipe his nose. "And then," he continued, "I guess I'm going to have to learn how to cook."

I laughed. "What about Shelagh?"

"I put in a call to my lawyer. We're looking into an annul-ment. It's a bit unusual after so many years of marriage, but under the circumstances—"

"I hope that works out."

"Well, I'd best be off. Got a drive ahead of me." He stood and looked down at me. "I've been thinking, since I found out

Olivia had been pregnant, that I'd like to give the baby a name. So when I go out there to talk to them, I can address it properly. I don't know if it was a boy or a girl so I thought a name that could be used for both might be a good idea. If it hadn't been for you and Detective Jeffers, I might never have gotten my family back. So with your permission, I'd like to call my child Jamie. After you."

"Oh, Duck, I'd be honored."

I watched him walk heavily over to his truck, reaching once again for the handkerchief. His shoulders gave a heave and he steadied himself against the door before stepping up into the cab. He sat there for a long time, staring at the theatre, and when Moustache and I pulled out of the driveway, he was staring still.

CHAPTER 44

I could see the back of his head as I descended the stairs. I had been in no hurry to get up. Although I had been given the green light by the hospital, I was still a little weak after my ordeal, and the show the night before had exhausted me more than I had thought possible. I had no idea how long he had been sitting there.

"What are you doing?" I asked, opening the front door.

Jeffers smiled and held up two paper bags. "I brought breakfast."

He pushed by me into the house. Moustache came barreling down the hall at the scent of food.

I was wearing bright yellow fleece pants, a white, off-the-shoulder sweatshirt over a purple tank, and my red Crocs. My hair was a mix of bed head and wig head and as I self-consciously ran my fingers through the tousle, I realized that everything Jeffers and I had been through had brought us to a level where things like that didn't matter. We had seen each other at our best, not just physically, and we had witnessed moments that were not our finest and we had arrived at that comfortable place where anything goes and all is forgiven.

He deposited his wares on the counter and made a grand fuss over Moustache, who wiggled and jumped, mouth open in an unmistakable smile. I found myself mirroring the dog's grin. Moustache loved Jeffers and so did I. Having spent so much of my life shutting people out or keeping them at bay, I was amazed how good it felt to open my heart. Olivia, Jeffers, Adam, and even Jarod Riley had all finagled themselves in there and, for the first time since my childhood, having friends was not such a terrifying prospect.

"Did you rob a buffet?" I asked.

Jeffers was laying out container upon container of the most amazing breakfast—smoked salmon, eggs Benedict, thick slices of peameal bacon, hash browns, croissants, a spinach, red pepper, and goat cheese quiche, fresh fruit salad, and two wedges of chocolate cake on which something I was unable to make out was written in white icing.

"Sort of," he said. "Aria's sister was having a surprise baby shower-brunch this morning. I, of course, was not invited because, as I'm sure you know, husbands don't really have anything to do with their wives getting pregnant. So when I dropped Aria off among all her lady friends, I protested my exclusion with Tupperware."

I applauded his coup and let Moustache out the back door. He went begrudgingly, set a world record for the fastest pee, and was back with his nose pressed against the window. I let him in and he ran to his dish, only to be disappointed by his usual fare.

"We have some celebrating to do," Jeffers said, pulling out a bottle of cheap sparkling wine and a can of frozen orange juice. "I hope you have a jug."

He plated and reheated the food while I prepared the mimosas and soon we were settled in the living room, enjoying the spoils of Jeffers' heist. Moustache kept a hopeful eye on us.

"So what are we celebrating? Did Shelagh finally confess?"

"No, she refuses to speak. She just sits there, shaking her head in denial. Erna Weins came down to give a statement about Shelagh's blackmail and what she *really* saw on the night of the murder. Handed over a big check, too. Turns out, she hasn't spent a cent of Shelagh's money."

"And Raines?"

"He's been cooperating fully. Even went in to talk to Shelagh. Thought he might be able to get her to talk. She went absolutely feral when she saw him. Had to be restrained. When I left last night, Morris was waiting for Psych to come and get her."

"What does that mean?"

"It means that Mrs. Worthy is going to be spending the next little while undergoing a psychiatric evaluation. What comes of that will determine the nature of her trial."

"Don't tell me there's a chance she could get off because of mental instability?"

"No way. We have more than enough evidence against her. Don't worry about that. No, what's up in the air is whether Shelagh spends the rest of her days in general population or in the mental disability unit. As for Raines, he's in for a long road," Jeffers continued around a mouthful of food. "A criminal investigation. A departmental investigation. Could take years. At the moment he's assisting the investigation as best he can, but once the focus shifts to his part in the whole thing, I don't know. Frankly I wouldn't be surprised if he ate his gun."

"Why do you say that?"

"The guy was set to retire in two months. Now he's been disgraced, his pension is being withheld pending the investigation, his whole career is in shadow, and there's no question as to his guilt. The only questions out there are how many laws did he actually break and how much jail time will he get? Cops don't do well inside. What would you do?"

"So," I said, changing the subject, "what are we celebrating?"

Jeffers reached into his pocket and placed his badge and I.D. card on the couch between us. "Major Crimes. Officially."

"Oh, Jeffers. Congratulations! Aria must be so relieved."

"I don't think she'll be relieved until I'm stuck behind a desk or retired, but yeah, she's pretty happy."

"I know how badly you wanted this. I'm so happy for you."

"There's still the divisional review to get through. Looks like my suspension will coincide with the baby's birth and some of Aria's mat leave, so that's a plus. My sole focus can be on Aria and our little boy. Honestly, I can't imagine anything better."

I had completely forgotten the review would be right on the heels of this case closing. My face fell.

"Hey, it's all good," he said. "Morris assures me that it will be relatively quick and painless. They've got their hands full with Raines, and his interference with the investigation makes some of my actions more justifiable. I'm by no means off the hook, but I know I have a job waiting for me when it's all said and done."

I guessed there were other officers who might blame their actions on Raines entirely, but Jeffers had done wrong and had broken rules and was not afraid to accept the responsibility and the reprimand that came with it.

"I'm proud of you," I said.

"We make a good team, Samuel."

I laughed. "I can't believe I'm going to say it but I'll miss this."

"What? You think that's it? One case and you're done?"

"What are you talking about?" I asked, still laughing.

"I deputized you. Remember? Plastic sheriff's badge and all! That's for life."

"I'm not sure you'll be able to convince Morris to let me—"

My words were cut off by a loud banging outside, to which Moustache lent his voice. From the front window I could see a man hammering a large post into my lawn.

"Can I help you?" I asked, opening the front door and coming onto the porch.

"Sorry, ma'am. Didn't mean to disturb. Name's Big Dave.

Niagara Real Estate." He handed me a card. "I'm just dropping off the sign. I know the office mentioned I'd be by this afternoon, but my schedule filled up so it was easier to swing by now. I hope that's okay."

I didn't know what he was talking about. There was a FOR SALE sign leaning up against his car. The sign displayed the Niagara Real Estate logo and their slogan—*"Turning Houses into Homes for over Fifty Years."*

I looked from the sign to the post and back to Dave, who was smiling. "The Festival is selling the house?" I asked.

"Actually, the Shaw rents the house from a couple up in Bracebridge. They inherited it when the wife's mother died several years ago and have been renting it to the theatre. They thought they might eventually retire out this way but now . . ." His smile remained but he crinkled his nose. "With everything that's happened, they think it might not be the right place for them."

I considered their position. As the owners of the house, they would have been informed and questioned about the bones, and they were obligated to disclose the information to potential buyers. I wondered if their desire to sell was the result of being legitimately spooked or trying to cash in on the moment and attract the kind of person who was willing to pay big bucks for the macabre novelty of the place.

"I imagine it will go the way of most of the old cottages around here. Torn down and replaced with something bigger." Dave fastened the sign to the hooks on the post. "I should only be a few more minutes."

"Take your time," I said, starting back into the house. *Turning Houses into Homes for Over Fifty Years.* "Out of curiosity," I said, "what are they asking?"

CHAPTER 45

"You bought the house?" Natalie squealed.

"Nothing's official yet. I'm still waiting to see if they'll accept my offer."

"They're going to accept. Who are you kidding? You offered them asking price!"

I hadn't squabbled about their closing date, either. The sellers were truly uneasy about the property and wanted to unload it as quickly as possible. They had priced it unbelievably low in the hope of a quick sale. Under normal circumstances, the size of the lot and its proximity to the water would have netted a price tag well beyond my means, but the sellers believed the house's history would overshadow the property's true worth and they let it go for a song. One I could afford. Terri-Mae had seen to that.

"We'll know by six tonight so, until then—"

"I never thought you, Bella James, would ever settle."

Natalie had the enthusiasm of ten people and once she got started, there was no slowing her down. She drove me crazy, but I smiled as she prattled on.

The last time we spoke I had just returned home from the hospital. She topped the list of people to whom I owed my life and our telephonic reunion had been rich with emotion. This conversation was very different and, although I was reluctant to celebrate too soon, I relished her abandon.

"We'll need to get you some proper furniture before we even

think about having a housewarming party," she said, "and I'm going to talk to Zack about painting a piece for you. It is so important to have some original art!"

I inhaled deeply and let it out slowly. Making the offer had been impulsive and every minute since had been filled with second guessing. But try as I might to talk myself out it, I couldn't. The history that had frightened away its owners was the very thing that drew me in. The pure and simple fact was, I could not bear the thought of someone else buying this house and this land only to tear it down and dig it up. This was my home. The *only* thing Terri-Mae had ever wanted to give me. And now she had.

I was driving myself crazy waiting for the phone to ring. Natalie had succeeded in her efforts to get me excited about the house, which made waiting for the official acceptance excruciating. It had rained most of the morning and the grass still glistened with moisture. Normally, I would have held off on walking the dog until it had dried up some but the sheer nervous energy propelled me out the door, leash in hand, and Moustache in tow.

The only off-leash area in Niagara-on-the-Lake is a long dirt path located in the Commons—the grounds of old military barracks close to the center of town. It was the only place I felt safe to let Moustache off his lead. I knew it would be muddy and that I'd regret bringing him, but I needed the distraction and he deserved a good romp.

He started tugging as soon as the path came into view. I unclipped his leash and watched him waggle up the lane, lifting his leg every couple of steps. His need to sniff every blade of grass that lined the pathway made him easy to overtake and I was well ahead of him when I heard the scuffle.

I turned to find Moustache trading snarls with a Golden

Retriever while a poor man struggled to intervene. I got a grasp on Moustache's collar at about the same time as the man took hold of the retriever, but the big dog's momentum caused the man to trip over himself and fall backward into a puddle.

"Oh my God! I'm so sorry. He hates retrievers. I never should have—"

Dr. Gorgeous looked up at me from the mud. My words froze mid-sentence and my hands flew to cover my gaping mouth and the laugh that escaped it.

"I'm glad you find this so amusing," he said, smiling.

"I'm so sorry," I said again.

He got to his feet and I cringed as I saw the whole of his left pant leg sticky with mud. Then I saw the bandage wrapped around the retriever's leg. I looked down at Moustache who was eyeing the retriever between intermittent growls.

"Stop it," I warned.

"No, it's okay. He just showing me he's feeling better," Dr. Gorgeous said, graciously, as he bent down to ruffle Moustache's mane.

Moustache transformed instantly from a vicious attacker to a professional dancer from *Fiddler on the Roof*. He danced in circles as Dr. Gorgeous scratched his ears and patted his rump. The retriever looked on but said nothing.

"I've been thinking about you," Dr. Gorgeous said, looking at me then quickly back to Moustache. "I wanted to call but—"

"Moustache isn't very good about answering the phone."

"How are *you* feeling?"

"We are both back to our old selves."

"That's what a doctor loves to hear."

There was a bit of an awkward pause as I wrestled with wanting to open up to him about our ordeal but not knowing if that was getting too personal.

Instead, I settled for, "Is your dog okay? I see the bandage. I hope Moustache didn't—"

"She's fine. She's not mine. I'm just taking her out for some fresh air. Giving her a chance to stretch her legs. She had some surgery on her hip a few days ago and I wanted to see how she would do with a bit of a run." He stroked the retriever's head. "And don't be fooled," he went on. "Shelby is not the harmless victim in this situation. I think the only one who's coming out of this the worse for wear is me." He chuckled and pulled at where his pant leg had stuck to his skin.

"Please let me pay to have them cleaned."

"There are scrubs back at the office. And this is nothing a washing machine can't take care of. I'll probably be able to brush most of it off by the time I walk to the clinic." He checked his watch. "I have to get her back."

The retriever must have sensed a change in the tension of the leash because she took a few steps in the direction they had come. Dr. Gorgeous followed the dog's lead. Moustache gave a snort and looked up at me.

Dr Gorgeous turned around to face me but continuing walking backwards, "If you really want to make it up to me, you could take me for a drink. I'll be done around seven."

My stomach felt like it was under attack by an army of butterflies. "What about Manda?"

I was sure whatever I had done to Manda's robe would be done to me a thousand times over if she thought I was moving in on her territory.

"What *about* Manda?" he said, coming to a halt.

"I thought you and she were—"

"Me and Manda? She's a nice lady. She offered me tickets to a couple of openings. There's nothing else."

The butterflies upped their efforts and I felt the corners of my mouth curving upward.

"Okay then," I said, the smile fully formed. "Seven sounds great."

He gave the retriever a little click and started off at a slow jog. Another snort from Moustache. If it's possible for a dog to look smug, Moustache was doing it.

"Did you snarl at the retriever on purpose?" I asked my dog.

Moustache gave a shake before trotting off down the lane. I followed behind him. Three feet off the ground.

ABOUT THE AUTHOR

Alexis Koetting lived in Niagara-on-the-Lake for over a decade and she knows the streets of that little town intimately. She currently resides in Hamilton, with her husband and pup (from whom she gets all her inspiration for Moustache). Alexis holds a BFA with a Specialization in Theatre Performance from Concordia University in Montreal and an MSEd from Medaille College in Buffalo. She has been working as a Canadian actor for close to twenty years, appearing on stage at the Stratford Festival, the Watermark Theatre, The Sudbury Theatre Centre, The Lighthouse Festival Theatre, and many others. She has not appeared at the Shaw Festival . . . yet. *Encore* is Alexis' debut novel and the first book in the Bella James mystery series.